Without A Wolf

A Big Woods Pack Novel

Written by

Cara Roman

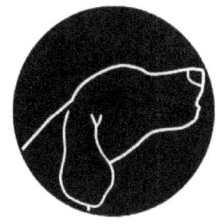

Baying Hound's Dark Side

USA

Disclaimers and Copyright

This book is a work of fiction. Names, characters, places, and incidents are the product of the author's imagination or, if real, are used fictitiously. Any resemblance to actual persons, living or dead, locales, or events is purely coincidental.

Without A Wolf

A Big Woods Pack Novel

Published by Baying Hound's Dark Side

ISBN: 978-0-9988282-7-5

Chapter 1

Greeted by a dreary gray sky and spindly trees naked of leaves Emma left work for the day. The weather had been unseasonably warm this week, or so she was told by everyone who came into the clinic she worked at. Having just moved to the northern Michigan town it sure felt plenty cold to her. Walking to her car she pulled her coat closed tighter as the wind kicked up almost knocking her down. Small piles of dirty slush from the melting snow coated the parking lot sloshing up onto the tops of her shoes soaking through the hem of her pants. Everyone always said how beautiful and perfect snow makes everything look, but what they forget to mention is how downright ugly it is if the weather gets above freezing for one day. The salt residue from the roads clinging to every available surface, including her black hatchback, making it look like it was going a little gray with age. She might have to look into a different car soon if she wanted to get through the winter in one piece. That thing basically skated everywhere on the slick roads, thankfully she only lived a few blocks away though. Being right in town wasn't usually ideal for her, with people crowding around, but she figured the advantage of being able to make it to work no matter the weather skewed the scales.

Tonight she was going to actually get out of the house. Emma was actually getting sick of her own company. She had been in town for a month now, and the only places that she has set foot in were the clinic, the grocery store, and her rental house. Since it came fully furnished, including pots and pans, she hadn't even had to venture the twenty minutes north in search of a big box store. Heading home to change out of the scrubs and find somewhere to eat dinner that was not at the kitchen counter watching reruns should be a big improvement. Maybe then some of the other nurses would stop trying to set her up with this available cousin, or that single neighbor. Thinking to herself that maybe she should have made up a story about a heartless ex-fiancé that left her at the altar and then nobody would try to foist her off on every unclaimed guy in the town. Lying came easily, but having the skill and wanting to use it are completely different. Dad taught her long ago that just because you are able to do something doesn't mean you have the right to.

The five-minute drive home was just long enough to fit in one full song on the radio, unless there is a commercial playing. She turned into the drive at the small white house with chipped paint and the scrolled wrought iron front porch just as the last notes of the country song faded. Thankfully being January meant Christmas music wasn't clogging every single radio station anymore. The holiday season lost a lot of its magic when you were all alone. Shaking her head reminding herself not to get into a negative funk again, since it was a whole year away. Grabbing the mail from the box on the side of the house as she unlocked the door. Ahhhhh, toasty warm, perks of that programable thermostat the landlord seemed so proud of. Having the heat kick on thirty minutes before she walked in the door was quite appreciated in this chilly climate though. All of the mail was addressed to 'current resident', nothing new since there is nobody to mail letters she chucked the small stack into the trash bin.

After swapping the blue scrubs for regular clothes, she headed back out. The last streaks of sunset painting the sky in hues of pink and orange. Emma headed to the bar just south of the town limit sign, since she was told the other day from a coworker that the food was pretty good. The inside of Dusty's Roadhouse was divided into three sections. A row of booths along the back wall with a half dozen round tables situated in front of them. Along the side opposite the door was a bar with beer taps and bottles of liquor sitting on the mirrored shelves behind. The bar itself was one massive slab of wood polished until it shone with stools in front of it with seats of a padded brown leather. The very front of the open space held a small stage, and dance floor. Not surprisingly that particular space was empty of people since it was a weeknight, and only just now six pm. A swinging door opened from next to the bar and a small, slim waitress with short dark hair rushed out carrying a tray full of food for the group of women seated at one of the booths. The place was about half full, and since there didn't seem to be any hostess stand she chose one of the small tables toward the corner. The menu was already on the table, wedged in between the salt and pepper shakers, so she grabbed it and looking it over had just decided what sounded good when the waitress came over.

"You're a new face! Don't think I have seen you in here before. My name is Kayla!" The waitress said with a giant smile on her face holding her hand out to shake.

"Yep. Just moved here. I'm Emma," she replied shaking her warm hand. The touch of the waitress' hand zinging up her arm.

Kayla tilted her head to the side, her gaze narrowing the slightest noticing the sensation in her own arm. Clearly expecting her to elaborate further she said, "Its, ah, nice to meet you, what can I get for you?"

"I've heard everything here is pretty good, how about a burger with mushrooms and swiss cheese, steak fries and some ranch to dip them, oh and just ice water to drink please."

"Gotcha. I will go put that in, and be right back with your water," she said her nostrils flaring a beat before she smiled, but it this time it wasn't quite reaching her blue eyes.

While Kayla walked away her instincts were screaming. Oh, she knew what Kayla the waitress was alright, but there was no way she could just walk out now that she had placed an order, at least not without drawing attention to herself. Beating herself knowing she shouldn't have shaken Kayla's hand. She knew better, it had been drilled into her head from birth, but this time she didn't want to have to be rude damn it. Judging by the reaction she seen the woman couldn't quite gage what was different about her. Most of the time that was the case, and didn't that sting just as much as always. She knew she felt different to Kayla, but she couldn't smell the tinge of animal on Emma the way she could on her. Kayla was a wolf shifter, or as humans usually called them werewolves.

Two men walked in just then waving at Kayla walking over to Emma with her drink. Both of them were tall, with wide shoulders. Dressed in well-worn jeans, t-shirts and heavy work boots, with sharp steel blue eyes. But that's where the similarities ended. One was clean shaven with dark brown hair so long it flopped down over his ears. He had a big smile on his face. The other man was more guarded, his face set in serious lines. His eyes danced at the other man, but his mouth didn't crack a smile. His dark blonde hair was cut short on the sides, a little longer on top, and he had it pushed up and off his face. He had a full beard that just crossed the border from blonde to brown. There were dark streaks of ink down one arm, and the tattoo on the other arm peeked out of the short sleeve of his dark gray t-shirt. Clearly they were from the same genetic pool, brothers or at the very least first cousins. Thinking to herself that was one pool well worth taking a dip in, and judging by the look on the faces of the women in the booth, Emma wasn't the only one admiring the view.

***

Kole was still laughing at his own stupid joke as they walked in. "When I was a kid I was scared of the dark, but now that I am an adult I am scared of the lights!" He was such a dumbass sometimes.

"Do ya get it Kian?' he asked.

"Yeah, I just don't think it's funny is all." It was a little funny, but he wasn't about to laugh at some idiotic joke about his brother's electricity bill.

"You would be in a better mood if you got your dick wet more often."

"This again? Can't we go one damn day without you worrying how much action I get?"

"Maybe if you got some in the last decade big brother!" Kole boomed out loudly, and laughing again.

A few heads turned, of course they heard Kole. They sat down on the bar stools and nodded at the bartender. He was reading an off-road magazine. But he knew they were here for Kayla so he didn't bother coming over to take their order. The place was only about half full right now, with most of the customers sitting at the tables to eat. Kayla walked up to the bar "How are my brothers tonight?" she said at normal volume, then whispering too low for anyone but them to hear as she grabbed them each a beer, "Lady at the table alone in the corner, she feels off."

Swiveling his head to check on her Kole asked "Off how?"

"Like a wolf. But I didn't smell anything but human on her, so I could be wrong," she answered.

Now Kian turned full around to look, and shit, she was a stunner. He completely forgot why he was looking and took a moment to just drink her in. An absolute ten on the scale, but you could tell she had no idea. Wavy auburn hair pulled back from her face twisted back into a clip, there were strands escaping to frame her face. Oh, what a face it was. High cheek bones with a small straight nose, a wide mouth with a slightly fuller bottom lip. There was a dusting of light freckles across the bridge of her nose and over her cheeks. Her eyes were down, and he couldn't see them through her mascara coated eyelashes as she looked at her phone. She had on a moss green sweater and dark jeans tucked into winter boots. Remembering why he was supposed to be looking at her, he sniffed the air, not noticing any of the rich smell that their inner animals all had. Shaking his head at his little sister that he didn't smell anything either.

Kole wiggled his eyebrows suggestively. "Want me to go introduce myself?"

"NO!" Kian said much louder than he meant to. He just couldn't stomach the thought of his brother making any moves on her. She looked up at the yell, and he was immediately caught in her gaze, helpless to look away. Her eyes were spectacular, seriously one of a kind. Her driver's license categorized them as hazel, but that hardly did the color justice. Dark forest green rimmed the outside, a light golden whiskey color in the center darkening back to green at her pupils. She blinked breaking the connection and he realized he hadn't been able to breathe while looking at her. Nobody in all his 30 years had ever affected him like that.

The bell from the kitchen chimed to let Kayla know an order was up, and she disappeared into the kitchen. Kole was looking at him like he had grown a second head, so he turned back around and took a swig of the beer his sister had brought over. Keeping his eyes on the beautiful stranger in the mirror. She looked a little shaken at the shared moment too. Kayla walked out with a single plate on her tray and headed straight over to the beauty.

"Here ya go Emma, burger with mushrooms and swiss, and ranch for your fries. So, just moved here huh? Are ya looking for work? We have a lazy waitress that still hasn't made it in tonight even though her shift started an hour ago."

Around a nibble of fry Emma said, "Oh, umm, thank you, but no. I work at the clinic, I'm a nurse."

"Oh, nice! That's too bad for me though, it would have been nice to replace her. Enjoy your dinner, and just yell if you need anything." Kayla said the last part as she was walking off.

Kian could tell that Kayla still couldn't tell what was off about Emma. Either he was going to have to watch Kole hit on her, or think of some reason to go over there and size her up by himself. Her voice was lower than he would have expected, a mellow alto instead of a ringing soprano. Smoky, and seductive, just the sound of it had his dick at half-mast like he was a teenager again getting a boner if the wind changed directions, instead of a grown man. *Son of a bitch*, he thought to himself, *that woman was going to be trouble!*

Chapter 2

The blond man watched Emma as she ate her dinner. The food was just as great as she had been told, but she couldn't enjoy it with that sexy stranger eyeing her the whole time. She could feel those eyes on her even without looking up. He probably thought she didn't notice since he was staring into the mirror instead of directly at her. Like some cruel joke, there was nothing wrong with her instincts, and they were screaming at her right now. But Emma knew better than to run from a predator, so she took her time, trying to eat at a normal pace. Checking her phone like she was playing a game, constantly chanting *'just act normal'* inside her head.

Not surprisingly Kayla hadn't brought the check over. She clearly wanted Emma to come up to the bar to pay so her brothers could get a closer look. *Didn't that just figure though? Go out one night for dinner and end up stumbling across three shifters.* Her father always told her that others of their kind wouldn't be accepting of a shifter without a wolf inside. She had no animal for protection making her too fragile for their way of life. Hopefully as long as they didn't touch her then the three siblings would just assume Kayla had gotten an electric shock and nothing more. Once could be explained away as a coincidence, but not if it happened again.

Putting her coat on, and gathering up her purse she headed towards the bar, aiming for the end away from the beefcake brothers. The little smile at her nickname for them fell once Kayla waved her over though. She was standing behind the bar in front of her brothers. Left with no other options, Emma changed direction. The brunette one leaned back past his brother's head and gave her a big smile as she approached. Oh, he was a charmer, she was sure the ladies all dropped their panties as soon as he looked in their direction. It didn't escape her notice that they herded her exactly where they wanted her, right next to the blonde man, who was clearly the eldest. He was still taller than her while seated on the stool making her feel unusually petite.

"Hey! How was everything?" Kayla asked bringing her order up on the cash register's screen behind the bar.

"Good, thank you," Emma said nodding her head.

"These are my brothers, Kole, and Kian."

"I'm Kole the dashingly handsome brother," he said his hand on his chest with a wicked smirk and wink.

"Kian," said with a jerk of his chin, and eyes that had frosted over.

"Nice to meet you," Emma said breathing a tiny sigh of relief neither had shaken her hand.

"Oh, its mighty slippery out there right now. All that melted snow from earlier froze and I haven't gotten a chance to sprinkle salt just yet," Kayla said looking pointedly at her brothers. "Wouldn't want your first time here to end in a spill outside."

"Oh, I'll be careful, no worries," Emma said backing away.

Without a word Kian stood up following her towards the door. Grabbing the handle just as Emma was about to reach for it he held the door open for her. Guiding her through the doorway with a light touch on her back he said, "Ladies first."

She felt his touch burn through her heavy winter coat, sweater, and all the way down into the marrow in her bones. He must be very dominant to give off so much power with one small touch. Instead of freezing in fear though, her body was begging to burrow in for more. All the nerve endings in her body felt shockingly alive, and she was instantly wet between her legs. No, no, no. Absolutely not! Her hormones weren't in charge of the show, damn traitors anyway, with considerable effort she stepped away putting much needed distance between them. He was still standing there just outside of the doors, as she headed to her car.

Emma needed to get away from the way Kian had made her feel. Hands shaking as she put the key into the ignition starting the little car and put it into gear. As she pulled out of the parking lot onto the road she braved a glance at him in the rearview mirror. She expected him to be staring at her since she was unashamedly fleeing from him now. But he was gazing at his hand in shock. Strange. Didn't he know his own power by now?

***

Kian let off a rumbling growl, he could still feel Emma on his hand. Like he stole a little of her aura by touching her, but was too greedy to give it back. No doubt about it. She was definitely not human. She felt like more, much more. It hadn't escaped his notice that she didn't trip or slip once as she jogged across the icy parking lot. Nobody had ever set his entire body on fire like that. His dick was pressing so hard on the inside of his zipper it might break free at any minute. One fucking touch and he was already halfway there. That was only supposed to happen when two animals who were fated connected. His wolf was pacing back and forth inside. Nervous that he was letting her get away. He wasn't looking for a mate, especially one who smelled so fragile and human. *Mate, she is our mate*, his wolf said. Shaking his head at how complicated his life just became Kian walked back inside.

Kole was standing his back leaned against the bar waiting for him. He lifted an eyebrow in question.

"Fuck man, I don't know what the hell she is. But my wolf thinks she's meant for me." Kian grabbed his beer gulping the rest of it down like those words had burned to admit out loud.

They both stood there for a few minutes letting it sink in. Rubbing a hand across his square jaw Kole finally said, "Can't be. She would have felt it too. It's probably just been too long for you. Right?"

"From the way her eyes went wide and the

pheromones pouring off of her she did."

"Aww hell, man. This isn't gonna be good. You know how our uncle feels about wolves mating with humans. It's against the fucking rules for a reason Kian, they usually can't handle it, and get hurt. Sure, Emma is a knockout, but there are women in the pack that you should take out if you're ready to settle down."

"None of them ever made me hard with a single touch like she just did. Fuck. Just let me figure this shit out, don't mention it, okay?" Kian asked setting money down on the bar to cover his tab.

Kayla walked over just as Kian was heading back out the door.

"So, what happened with Emma?" she asked Kole.

"Nothing good Kay, nothing good," Kole said eyes still on the door from which Kian just left.

"Is she a wolf Kole? You know we are supposed to report any rogues to the Alpha so he can check them out," she whispered.

"No wolf, don't worry about it," Kole said careful not to actually lie to his sister as he settled back down on a stool.

Kian drove around town in his truck for an hour before giving in and looking for Emma's car in a driveway. If she had a garage maybe he would just have to shift and sniff her out. She smelled delicious, like green apples, and vanilla. That could be dangerous though, someone might notice a wolf strolling around town. Getting shot in the ass wasn't how he wanted to end his night. Just as he was admitting to himself that he was definitely a certified creeper he saw the little black car sitting next to a tiny white house. He drove past going to the end of the block before circling around to make a slower pass. This time he knew for sure it was her place because the lights inside were on, and Emma was pacing back and forth in the living room. Probably wondering what the hell happened back in the parking lot. The look on her face pulled him in though, he could tell she was going to leave, and he couldn't let her run away.

Without A Wolf

Chapter 3

Emma heard the knock on the door just as she was heading from the living room into the bedroom. Intent on packing her clothes and leaving this town tonight. Nobody had knocked on her door since she moved in. She knew it had to be Kian, the shock in his eyes as she pulled away flashing through her mind. The urge to flee was instant, but there was no way to get to her car without having to go past him. With his senses she damn sure couldn't sneak past, and had no hope of outrunning him. He could shift in an instant and chase her for miles without tiring. Emma was a good runner, had taken all the self-defense classes she could, but she was no match for Kian's wolf.

"Emma? It's me." Thinking he was a dumb fuck for saying me he corrected, "Umm Kian, from the bar, I walked you out." Wincing at what a fool he was making of himself. Taking a deep breath to settle, "I just wanted to talk to you a minute." That was better, at least it didn't sound like this was his first time talking to a woman.

"Like I am supposed to believe that and open the door to you? I don't know you Kian. I think you should go home," Emma shouted from deep inside the house.

Thinking good mate, keeping herself safe. "Look, we both know what I am. But you should know that I'm not here to hurt you, I don't even know what you are." Once the words started rolling out they didn't stop, and he admitted, "I just need to know what you felt when I touched you. Because I have never felt that spark with anyone else." Voice getting lower now and almost pained, "Emma, you lit me up."

Well shit, her gut told her that was all truth. Not scared anymore, just pissed off that she had to leave a town she just moved to, she opened the door and glared up into his face, "I am leaving tonight, I won't be here much longer so you are going to have to find someone else to catch fire with

Kian whatever the hell your last name is."

He smiled, and it did her in. A little lopsided but with straight white teeth, small crinkles at the corners of eyes that said he used to smile all the time. The frost was all gone, and those eyes shone a clear blue now. He was sexy as all hell before, but that smile transformed his whole face. He radiated warmth, and Emma's knees went weak just looking at him.

Laughing at her he said "Kian Decker, Second to the Alpha, Big Woods pack." Then sounding more shy than a man who housed a dominant predator inside of him should be able to, "You are the most stunning woman I have ever seen in my entire life. Can I please come inside?"

Not sure what to say to that she just nodded and stepped aside to let him in. "Do you have a last name Emma?"

"Lowe. My last name is Lowe. I'm a nurse. No rank or pack to proclaim," she muttered still caught off guard by his smile.

Cocking his head to the side, "I hear the

truth ringing through your words, but I don't think that's all there is to it."

Eyes on the ground, wringing her hands, Emma took a deep breath and said something she had never admitted to anyone since her father died. "My parents were both shifters, but my DNA got confused somehow and I have no wolf."

"No wolf?" That couldn't be.

"Not so far, no." Emma said finally looking back up at him. Instead of the anger or disgust she was brought up to expect, she only saw confusion and then sadness in his eyes.

Reaching out he grasped her hand for a moment, his touch was just as potent as the first time "I know you feel that too. Do you know what that means?"

"That you must be a very powerful wolf. Shifters always feel like a little static shock to me."

"Yeah, I am, but that's not what that was. That's how it's supposed to be between mates who have been fated. Our animals connected, I felt you in every nerve of my body and I can smell how aroused just that small touch made you."

"Mates? How can I be anyone's mate when I am missing half of me? I have no animal for you to connect to Kian. I feel empty inside, like she should be there. But she just isn't." A tear escaped out of Emma's eye at her pained admission and raced down her cheek. Somehow, he didn't feel like a stranger anymore. He felt vital, like maybe her life was leading her to this exact moment.

Kian lifted his hand to her face, wiping the tear gently away. "I don't understand why you don't have a wolf, but I know I was meant to find you Emma. And now that I have I don't want to walk away from you."

Kian was so close, Emma leaned in, just to feel his warmth a minute. It should seem strange to her that just a few minutes ago she was ready to run, and now she wanted nothing more than to be in his arms. But it didn't, he was filling her senses and it was the best she had felt in a very long time. He smelled like animal, but also like man, deliciously spicy man. Her hands found their way to his chest and a soft rumble sounded from his throat. She didn't know that could sound so good. Looking up at him she whispered, "did you just growl at me?"

"Your touch makes me hungry for more." Kian said with another growl.

Feeling emboldened by his answer Emma ran her hands up from his chest over his shoulders and around his neck. "Me too."

Kian yanked Emma tight against his body. He was so much bigger than she was, taller by almost a foot, with shoulders almost too wide to fit through a doorway. He could literally break her, and suddenly Emma found that thought thrilling instead of scary. Feeling powerful in her vulnerability she rubbed her body against Kian's. His mouth crashed down on hers. His soft lips pressing against hers, his beard tickling her face. Needing more of him Emma sucked his bottom lip into her mouth, biting it gently. Kian's arms left her back, and for a heartbeat Emma thought he was going to push her away. Then she felt his hands sliding past her hips, down her legs, and catching just behind her knees picking her up as if she weighed nothing at all. Big strong wolf. Wrapping her legs around his waist she pulled back long enough to let him know, "First door on the right."

Kian left biting kisses along her jaw until he found her ear. He ran his tongue along the outside shell of Emma's ear as she let out a hungry little gasp. Encouraged that she liked that, Kian sucked the lobe into his mouth and then bit it scraping his teeth down it instead of just releasing it. Body on fire now, Kian set her down next to the bed, and leaned back enough to pull his shirt off. The tattoos Emma had caught peeking out of his sleeves earlier were magnificent. One whole arm was covered, across his chest, and down almost to the elbow of his other arm. And what a chest it was, muscular pecks, a deep indentation between with a sprinkling of light brown hair. Kian had eight pack abs and a sexy strip of hair leading down into his pants. Pulling off her own sweater, and shimmying out of her jeans Emma let him see her lacy green bra and panties.

"They matched your sweater. Good lord woman. Look at you. Skin so soft, with enough curves to drive a man wild. Mine, it's all mine." Kian growled the last part as Emma bit down on the strip of muscles forming the sexy V of his hips, and undid the button on his jeans. Reaching down inside his boxer briefs she found his dick. It was already hard with skin so soft, like silk over steel. Taking him in one hand as she pushed his pants down with the other she stroked slowly from the base to the tip. He was so big that her fingers didn't touch while wrapped around him. She had to taste him, needing to have her mouth on him. Going down on to her knees she swiped her tongue across the tip. Looking up into his eyes she took as much as she could fit into her mouth. Kian's eyes lost all their blue, blazing silver now as he watched Emma's lips stretch around his dick. With her hand gripping the base she worked him slowly at first. Her mouth sliding up, twisting her tongue around the tip before sliding back down. Having Kian inside her mouth felt so good. Getting so turned on Emma squeezed her legs together.

Kian was going to come down her throat soon if he didn't stop her. Pulling his dick out of her mouth her lips making a little *pop* sound he pushed her back towards the bed. "Damn Emma, less than two minutes and I am already almost there, your mouth must be magic," Kian smirked. "My turn now."

Emma bounced back onto the bed and splayed her arms out to hold her head up so she could see. Opening her legs in hungry invitation she watched him lick his lips. Crawling to her he pulled the green lace aside and ran his tongue up her seam. Her breath caught and she clutched the comforter in her hands. Opening her legs wider with his arms he peeled back her lips to look at her. "Pussy so wet for me, and mmmmmm so good," Kian said right against her clit. His tongue lapping it once, twice, circling around it once, lapping twice, circling once. He set a devastating rhythm. Breathlessly gasping out nonsensical sounds her legs starting to shake. He pushed a finger inside her, his tongue never slowing down, his finger sliding back out, and a second one moved in with the first. The pressure was building, she was gasping for breath now. His teeth grazed her clit once as his fingers pumped inside of her and on a cry Emma shattered. Her orgasm bowing her back up, pulsing greedily around his hand.

Kian smiled proudly at her, licked his fingers once before pulling her panties down her legs. Settling his knees between her legs he pulled her up to meet his mouth. Emma could taste her heady flavor on his lips, but it had felt so good she didn't have it in her to feel embarrassed. He reached behind her and she heard her lacy bra unsnap, pulling away he took the bra with him. Laying her back down he took a pink nipple in his mouth he pumped his dick slowly in his hand. Moving to the other nipple, sucking it hard into his mouth. Her nipple still in his mouth he said, "Stop me now Emma, if this is too fast for you."

Her hips rose in invitation, she moaned

"Don't you dare stop." He slid into her slowly, only halfway at first, stretching her. In again once more only halfway in. Finally on the third stroke he went in all the way until his hips met hers. He was so big, Emma had wondered if she could take him all. But she was so wet and needy from his mouth earlier that he slid in filling her completely. The muscle in Kian's jaw ticked as he pushed into Emma a little harder this time and she cried out. Lost in the sound of her pleasure he pounded into her harder and harder. She lifted her leg and he hooked it over his arm creating a different angle. God, Kian he was so close, his dick swelling. She was mumbling yes with every thrust, starting to quiver deep inside. He was growling, when she closed her eyes and her pussy clenched. Her orgasm triggered his, and hips pistoning into her he came. His dick jerking, warmth spilling into her as her aftershocks pulsed on.

Chapter 4

Kian wasn't ready to pull out of Emma just yet. His wolf craving that connection a little while longer. So he rolled them over draping her across his chest. Her hair clip was hanging halfway down her hair from their lovemaking. So he unclipped it freeing the wild red hair. Caught somewhere between curls and waves it tumbled halfway down Emma's bare back. Pulling one from the rest between his fingers he brought it to his nose inhaling the scent of fresh green apples. Smiling up at her he said, "I really like your shampoo."

Emma was tracing patterns in his ink when she laughed at him. "Why thank you handsome wolf, I bought it because apples are my favorite fruit."

Kian kissed her lips with a smack. "Mmmmmm, mine too now. I want to know all of your favorites Emma, share all your secrets with me."

Giggling at him she replied, "Apples, country music, sappy books and funny movies. Hmmmm, quilted toilet paper, the color blue now, walks in the woods, pasta, oh and white wine, never red."

"Never red, I will keep that in mind. Blue now? Why did it change? What was it before?" Kian asked while running his fingertips up and down her back lazily.

"Your eyes. I get lost in them," Emma admitted with a small smile. "Tell me about you Mr. Kian Decker Second to the Alpha."

"Well, I'm thirty. My family owns a construction company, we mostly do repairs and renovations, but we do build an occasional house. I am the oldest, you met my brother and little sister. My friend Lex, he held me together when my Dad died about ten years ago. Mom finished raising us, and moved down south a few years ago. Staying in this pack was hard for her after he was gone, she couldn't move on."

"Both of my parents are gone too," She said quietly. "Mom died when I was a baby, and I don't remember her at all. My Dad left when I was twelve. We were living in a small-town Georgia at the time, he was gone when I came home from school one day. He didn't take anything with him but his truck and the picture of my Mom he kept on his dresser," Emma finished on a shrug. "I guess it was too hard being around me."

Heart breaking for his new mate Kian hugged her tight to his chest. "That must have been scary as hell for you."

"It was," Emma said into his chest. "All night I kept thinking he would come home, but he didn't. So the next morning I went into school and told my teacher my Dad was gone. With no other family I was placed in foster care. I bounced around the system until I aged out at eighteen."

"So your people are from down south?" Kian asked still holding her.

"No, I guess my Mom was from up north somewhere, I'm not really sure where. Dad was a rogue, said since his parents never settled into a pack he wouldn't even know how. He was born in Texas, but lived in just about every state. He told me that when he saw my Mom it was like the world just took a breath and the stars froze in the sky. Everything else faded away and his whole life centered on her like it was just the two of them, she must have felt it too since a few days later she ran away with him."

Nodding his head knowing exactly what that felt like now Kian kissed Emma's forehead. "They were mates fated to be together, like us babe."

"Does that mean you're gonna run away with me too Kian?"

Shaking his head, "I want you in my home Emma. To be a part of my pack."

"I don't know if I can, Dad told me that no pack would ever accept me. I'm bad luck, people would worry about their children being born empty inside like me, Kian. I can't defend myself with tooth or claw like the rest of you can. I have to leave now that I know there is a pack in this town, before they force me out. I want you to come with me." Eyes tearing up at the thought of leaving him after what they just shared together. "That was so much more than sex to me, I feel linked to you now."

"That's the way with mates. Our souls connected. Nobody else will ever be able to make you feel the same way I can. Soon you will be able to feel my emotions racing through you." Kissing her lips once, "I will keep you safe Emma. It's just us here tonight, but I would fight the whole world for you."

Thinking he just might have to do just that she leaned back down for another kiss. Feeling him growing hard inside of her again she licked past the seam of his lips. Tongue gliding playfully against his she moved her hips once. "I believe you, Kian." She sat up straight eyes locking on his glowing silver ones as she began to move up and down on him.

He gripped her hips growling out, "Mine, you're mine." Nodding her head on a moan she picked up the pace, hips rocking hard down onto him. Watching his beautiful woman ride his dick with such abandon was the sexiest thing he had ever seen. "My mate, fuuuuck, Emma. Mate. Tell me you're mine...say it." The rumbling growl constant now.

"Kian, oh god, I'm your mate Kian!" Emma shouted as the pressure built in her middle. She was so close already.

"Nobody but me." Kian was lifting his hips up slamming into her now. She arched her back, her full breasts with the pert little nipples pointing at the ceiling. Head tossed back hair tickling the top of his thighs as the first wave of orgasm rushed through her body. Emma was saying his name over and over with each ragged breath now, aftershocks pulsing on as his own orgasm shot into her in hot waves until it was more than she could hold and it dripped back down pooling onto him.

When their heartbeats slowed back down into a normal rhythm Kian laid Emma down next to him and went in search of the bathroom. Inside he cleaned himself up, rinsing out the washcloth he brought it back into her bedroom. "My wolf needs me to clean you," he explained.

"Okay?" Emma asked.

"You're mine to take care of now. You'll sleep better if you're not all sticky," he said as he ran the warm cloth ever so gently between her legs and over her thighs. "Shit Emma, I should have thought of protection, I will be more careful with you next time."

"I have been on the pill for years Kian. And you know we can't get diseases." She smiled sleepily at him. "I don't want anything between us Kian."

Her words had the wolf inside strutting proudly. *Our mate wants all of us.* Taking the washcloth into the basket in the bathroom Kian walked through the house checking the locks. He was a light sleeper by nature, and he told Kole not to say anything, but he wasn't taking any chances with his new mate. Emma wasn't human, but that didn't mean his Alpha would accept it. Kian would have to convince his uncle. That was a problem for tomorrow though. Tonight he was going to hold his beautiful woman while she slept. Lifting a sleepy Emma he pulled the sea blue comforter back, and settled them both between the sheets. She immediately draped a leg over his and curled into the crook of his arm.

"Kian?" she asked quietly.

"Yeah Em?" he replied.

"Tighter."

Kian pulled Emma tighter against him and listened to her breathing slow as she fell asleep. She smelled like him now. Apples, the vanilla he learned was from her lip gloss, and fur. As he drifted off into sleep he swore he was going to help her find her wolf if it was the last thing he did.

Chapter 5

After seeing Emma off at the clinic the next morning Kian drove his truck home to change his clothes, and pack a lunch for work. He lived a few miles north of town tucked into the woods on a long winding private drive. Most of the Big Woods pack lived on this road, the rest lived on either side along the road. His kind tended to live close together. Needing room to change and run as wolves, the forest provided sanctuary, and knowing the only neighbors were all pack meant the likelihood of some human stumbling upon them was slim. During deer hunting season they had to be especially careful though, not everyone respected no trespassing signs, and most of the county was out looking to fill their freezers and get that big ol' trophy buck up on the wall.

From there Kian headed straight to their

current jobsite, not bothering to head back into the office first. His uncle Russ would be there with their secretary Cathy, one of the older women in the pack. He handled most of the business end now, leaving Kian as the foreman to manage the guys on the crew, other members of the pack. Knowing he could get a full day in without having to see his stubborn Alpha gave Kian the time he needed to work out exactly how he was going to bring up what had happened. However, avoiding his brother wouldn't be possible since he worked the crew with him.

"Hey man, you're almost smiling today! Careful someone might think you finally fuckin' got a little something." Kole greeted Kian with an enthusiastic slap to the back.

"You smile enough for the both of us asshole. I actually have responsibilities in this pack," he returned with a shake of his head.

"Holy hell man, you actually did! I was just messin' with you, but you seriously did it! Shit, did you claim her?" Kole said, lowering his voice.

"Hell no I didn't! I wasn't sure what my bite would do to her. And I think it was enough of a shock about fated mates for her, shit Kole, she didn't know what that meant. Her parents didn't teach her much about her history other than to avoid us as a general rule. She was ready to bolt when I showed up."

"Leave it to you to chase your own mate away. I swear I got all the game in this family," Kole said rubbing his hands down his torso and rotating his hips suggestively.

"At least I found mine, tell me, exactly how many women have you sampled now little brother?" Kian replied putting him in his place.

"Hey, I'm not looking for a mate! Don't want one, ever," Kole said adamantly shaking his head, all the humor was gone from his eyes now.

"Ok, I will remind you of that if one ever falls into your lap." Kian laughed. "But seriously, can you get the fuck to work now? This god-awful bathroom isn't going to demo itself."

Snow had started falling as Kian sat in his

truck eating his sandwich. He took out his phone glad she had put her number in this morning before he left her. Texting her he said, *"Wanna come over to my place tonight? I'll pick you up in my truck... your little car would end up in a ditch halfway there."* Hitting send he smiled that she had programmed it in under 'Mate.' Like he would ever forget that, but her surprising possessiveness made his heart happy.

"Well aren't you rude this afternoon!? :p" Emma sent back.

"My apologies.....drive your car.....maybe I could be persuaded to drag you out with my truck when you get stuck. Your mouth is worth braving the elements. ;)"

His phone beeped. *"Perverted mate! I am wet imagining that though"* Before he could respond she followed that with a second text.

"Too bad you aren't here to take care of that for me. Maybe I will have to take care of that myself."

"That ain't playing fair woman!"

"But it is a lotta fun lol! I get out of work at five. Gotta go. Can't wait to see you Kian."

"Pack a bag. Miss you Em."

She sent him a kissy face back. He really did miss her. It had only been a few hours and already he was desperate to see her again. For the first time in his whole life he was wishing he didn't have the fast healing of his kind. He could go see her if he busted his thumb with a hammer. Shaking his head at how idiotic that sounded even to him he got out of his truck heading back to work. Wishing it would pass by quickly, but knowing it wouldn't since he had to update his uncle on the progress at the end of the day, and bring in paperwork from the jobsite. He wouldn't lie to him about finding a mate though, that felt too close to shame. And Kian could never be ashamed of Emma. She may think she needed a wolf to be strong, but he knew better. She had to have had a spine of steel to make something of her life after her past. Putting herself through school to become a nurse, not to mention picking up and starting over town after town. Kian had no idea what it would have been like growing up without a rock-solid support system.

Calling it a day Kian walked out of the house with the other guys on his crew. The work was hard, but he loved it. Making something out of nothing, or helping a place find its potential. He was leaving something of himself behind in this town that would be around long after he was gone. Before he got in his friend Lex pulled into the driveway, getting out he strolled over to Kian's truck. "I heard some of the guys were talking about hockey this weekend if the ice on the lake is thick enough, you game?" Lex was a little shorter than Kian's own six-foot four-inch frame, though still intimidating in size. With dark brown hair that curled slightly, and warm brown eyes that Kane could read as well as if they were his own. They had grown up next door to each other. Played together as pups, pondered the mysteries of girls together through puberty, and beaten each other bloody a few times along the way.

Shaking his head he smiled, Kian pulled the

sweat soaked white t-shirt off wiping it his face on it. "Nah man, I'll pass. Got some plans already."

"Yeah right. With who, Kole is already in, and Kayla has to work," Lex said giving his shoulder a shove. Kian didn't answer just kept buttoning the flannel shirt he had changed into staring off towards town his blue eyes melting toward silver his friend took a small step back. "Come on man, it's me. What's up?" His voice serious now.

"I know, you are as much family to me as Kole, or Kayla."

"Then what the hell man?"

"Shit." Pausing to run his hands through his dirty blond hair. "I met my mate. And she's incredible, smart, she has all this wild red hair, with freckles," Kian said.

"Son of a fucking A! Congratulations man!" Lex beamed at him with excitement for a minute, but feeling Kian's stress his grin faded. "Tell me she isn't human though Deck." Using the nickname he gave him all those years ago. "The Alpha is going to flip. He's always been against bringing humans into our pack. He'd never let you turn her."

"She isn't, she is a born shifter. But it's complicated."

Lex raised an eyebrow in silent question for him to continue.

"She doesn't have a wolf inside. Can't shift," Kian finally admitted.

"Good luck with that, it may be a problem for Russ, which is fucked up. But I think it's great, I can't wait to meet her. See you later man, let me know if you change your mind about the game, she might wanna watch you lose!" Lex called the last part walking towards his own truck.

Knowing that both Kole and Lex were happy for him put Kian in a better mood as he drove to the office. They had always had his back, no matter what. Kian noticed that Cathy's car wasn't in the lot anymore. She usually left early on Friday. Good, that way he wouldn't have an audience when he talked with his uncle. She was the biggest gossip in the whole pack, which is probably why Russ had her as a secretary. She let him know everything going on. Taking a deep breath to settle the animal pacing inside of him he pushed the door open.

Russell Decker sat behind the desk in his office. He was still a good-looking man in his early fifties, shifters tended to age well since all of the environmental free radicals had no effect on them. His trimmed brown hair going gray up the sides. With eyes the same steely blue all of the Decker's had. He was tall and wide, although not as much as Kian. That didn't matter thought, he was always a hard man. Which made Kian wonder if it was because he had never been mated. As Alpha Russ expected his pack to fall in line no questions asked. Kian's own father had actually been older by a year, but he had been stayed Second to his powerfully dominant Alpha brother. Looking up as Kian entered he called out, "Kian my boy, a few minutes late today. That's not like you. Snow must be coming down harder out there than I thought."

Handing the folder holding the paperwork over he said, "Lex needed to talk to me a minute."

"Everything alright with Deputy Kolter?" Russ said using Lex's official title.

"Yeah, but there is something you should know." His uncle steepled his hands atop the desk waiting for Kian to continue. "I found my mate."

"Within our pack?"

"No, she was eating dinner at Dusty's when I went in for a beer last night," Kian said, careful with the words he chose.

"You mated to a human?" His Alpha's eyes narrowed and the power in the room ticked up a notch.

"She was born a shifter Uncle Russ, but her wolf is hidden somewhere deep inside," Kian said still standing on the other side of the desk. This wasn't the kind of thing you said sitting down.

"Well that is unusual." Thinking a moment, he went on. "Tell me about this mate of yours. What pack does she come from?" The power fading down now.

"Her name is Emma Lowe, she is a nurse at the clinic. No pack, her father was a rogue. Her mother belonged to a pack but ran away with him. She died when Emma was too young to remember her. When her Dad took off on her at twelve and she ended up in the foster care system." Kian knew Russ wasn't asking about how funny she could be, or the way her eyes looked like sunlight streaming through the branches in the forest.

Finally his uncle said, "Congratulations are in order. Bring her to the pack meeting Sunday so I can see her for myself."

"I will, and maybe someone in the pack will have an idea about her wolf."

"Go on then, I have some business that needs taking care of before heading out," Russ said.

Chapter 6

Dawn was just starting to lighten Kian's bedroom. His warmth was pressed up against her back, his strong arms around her. Emma's body felt deliciously used, and she smiled to herself remembering everything they had done to make it sore. Kian was a man born to please a woman. Tall, stacked with muscle, a big thick dick, nimble fingers and a clever tongue that he used to worship her body, drawing orgasm after shocking orgasm from her. She lost count how many times he had taken her there this weekend. Like addicts starved for each other they had had sex on his couch, on his kitchen counter, up against the wall in the shower, and in his bed over and over again. Somehow each time he filled her felt even better than the last.

As good as the sex with him was, and she was considering taking a billboard out to let everyone know how well and thoroughly ravished she was, Emma was amazed at the man he was. Kian loved taking care of her, he claimed his wolf needed it, but she knew the man did too. Last night he made her delicious spaghetti and garlic bread because Emma had admitted it sounded really good to her. They ate it sitting on his big comfortable brown couch, him in boxers, while she wore only his t shirt. He had even kicked the heat in the house up on the off chance she might get cold. Emma had reminded him that although she couldn't shift she wasn't as frail as a human either. Kian had just smiled and adjusted the thermostat anyway. Emma was really falling hard for him.

Smiling as he stretched his big frame and rubbed his beard against the side of her neck she said, "Good morning my handsome wolf."

"Morning my sexy as hell mate," Kian replied kissing her shoulder blade rubbing his morning erection against her butt.

Emma was amazed at how turned on she was getting again. They had only finished collapsing exhaustedly into sleep a few hours ago. But she was soaking wet, and already absolutely desperate to have him inside of her. Moaning she guided his hand down between her legs.

"Always so wet for me Em, but I don't want to hurt you, we're having so much sex I'm surprised you can walk," Kian said as his finger rubbed back and forth on her clit.

Heartbeat pounding, she ground her hips into his hand. "I need you Kian, shifter healing, remember?"

Emma felt him smile against her neck and knew she had him. "Mmmmm, lucky me," he rumbled with his sexy gravelly morning voice. Kian slid into her slowly from behind, his fingers never stopping their movements on her needy clit. Setting the pace slow but deep she was gasping for air and moaning within moments. Reaching her hand behind her head her fingers grasping his hair she moved her hips back into him to meet his thrusts. Kian's growl vibrated against her throat, his teeth grazing her skin and Emma held her breath hoping he broke the skin to claim her. But his teeth eased up instead of biting down. Kian liked to tempt them both with those damn teeth of his.

His other hand moved up from gripping her hip to her breast. Kneading it and squeezing his fingers slightly, his palm rubbing against her sensitive nipple. Emma cried out shattering around him. Kian kept pumping into her, his fingers on her clit never stopping. Gripping his hand to stop the flood of sensations crashing into her body she whimpered, "Too much."

Kian shook his head pressing his fingers against her clit as his hips bucked into her slick wet heat faster and faster, his rhythm growing erratic the closer he got. The sensations were too much for her, almost bordering on pain. It was all Emma could do to keep herself breathing as her body began to shake. Kian groaned loudly at the first pulses of her second climax and holding her against him he buried his dick deep inside of her. The light seemed to fracture around them at the first spurts of his warmth within her, and Emma closed her eyes riding out the most intense orgasm she had ever felt.

Chapter 7

After their explosive morning in bed Kian went downstairs to make some breakfast while Emma showered. As much as he wanted to join her in there, and the thought of her naked and running her hands down her soapy body was almost killing him, through their strengthening bond he could tell she was nervous about the pack meeting. He figured giving her a little bit of space couldn't hurt. As a pup when he was upset, or something big was on his mind his mom had always made him French toast. His wolf demanded he feed and care for Emma, and French toast would help him settle too.

Kian's phone buzzed as he was setting the egged bread onto the skillet, picking it up he said, "Hey Kayla."

"Mmmmmhhhhmmmmm. Hey yourself big brother. So I have to hear it from Lex that you have mated? It was Emma wasn't it? Okay, good, good. I liked her ya know. She is pretty, polite, and brave approaching us at the bar to pay knowing what we were. I can't wait to spend some time with her!" Kayla said her moods changing from annoyance to excitement.

"Yeah Kay, she is amazing. Everything I wanted in a mate, and didn't know I needed."

"So she's a wolf then?"

"Not quite. She should have one, her parents were shifters, but for some reason she doesn't. We don't really know why. But Russ invited her to the pack meeting today, so maybe it won't be a big deal," Kian said while flipping the French toast. He was trying to convince himself just as much as his sister.

"Yeah, I really don't know about that Kian. I don't care what she is so long as you are happy. Love you, see you two there!" Kayla had a whirlwind personality.

Smiling to himself at his soul-deep happiness he plated Emma's breakfast as she walked in smelling like an orchard. Kian hoped that his house always smelled like this from now on, his fur, her apples. Emma wore a dark blue sweater over light jeans today. Her hair waving wild and crazy around her face. Wanting to make a good impression she had put on makeup for the first time all weekend. Her lashes were darker, and her lips glossed up. She settled on the stool at the island and he set the steaming plate of French toast on the granite countertop in front of her with a smile.

"Orange juice, or coffee m'lady?" Kian asked with a lopsided grin.

The tension left Emma's face as she laughed. "Orange juice today, I think you woke me up plenty."

Getting her juice his wolf nodded proudly inside. *We please our mate.* He made his own French toast as she poured syrup over hers and ate. Once his heaping stack was done he sat down next to her and dug into his own plate. Neither one of them spoke until all the food was gone, comfortable just to be near one another. Getting up to help load the dishes into the dishwasher Emma said, "I love your house Kian. Dark wood floors and cabinets, with the tall ceilings, light gray walls, all this stainless steel. Knowing what you do for a living I'm not surprised its nice, but I didn't expect to feel so at home here."

"I like to be comfortable. I'm a big man, so big rooms with big furniture made sense. I like how it feels with you here." Hoping she liked it enough to call it her home soon too.

While they cleaned the kitchen up Kian explained about the pack meeting to Emma. That they were usually at the Alpha's house, everyone usually gathered in the back yard. Any important issues were discussed, any challenges for rank within the pack were held. Sometimes they ran as a pack together, but not always. These days Russ was more about leadership than time spent bonding together, but Kian remembered how different it was before his Dad died. Once the kitchen was spotless Kian asked if Emma was ready to go.

"As I will ever be I guess," she shrugged halfheartedly.

The Alpha was one of the furthest neighbors out, a couple miles from Kian's house, but the drive only took a few minutes. Not nearly enough time for second thoughts. Russell Decker had a large house of dark wood siding and big windows. Although it was sturdy looking and well-kept there wasn't much curb appeal, or a welcoming feeling. The driveway and most of the front yard was full of cars and trucks, most everyone was there already. Kian parked his big truck just off the road right next to a white and gold police cruiser. Noticing Emma's look of shock as they got out, he explained that his friend Lex was with the county sheriff's department, and probably just getting off shift. Walking through the snow around the side of the Alpha's big house Kian could hear everyone talking excitedly at once about the Second finding his mate. Taking a deep breath, his arm already around Emma, he pulled her even tighter against his side as everyone quieted at their approach. With a final smile for his mate they turned the corner.

The back yard was just an opening into the woods. And it was filled with the entire pack. Shifters of all ages, about twenty of them, and all eyes were on Kian and Emma as they made their way to the back porch where Russ liked to stand and preside over his people. Kian heard the sharp intake of breath each person took as they walked past, and he knew it was because Emma smelled completely human to them. The excitement turned sharply into suspicion. Feeling her shame streak through the bond he squeezed her waist letting her know he was with her, and that it was ok. Just as they reached the steps Russell Decker stood up and announced to the pack.

"Welcome Big Woods Pack, as you may have heard our Second has apparently stumbled upon his fated mate. As your Alpha I introduce you to Emma Lowe, unclaimed mate to my nephew Kian Decker."

"But she is human, it's against your own rules Alpha," a man from the back yelled angrily.

People had been cast out as rogues for mating with humans.

Before Russ could say anything Kian turned around and said, "I understand the confusion, and bitterness some of you may be feeling. But let me assure you while Emma may smell human, she was born to shifter parents. My intent was not to break any rules, but to proudly show off my mate today, as any wolf would. That rule was made to protect our community from exposure. She is no threat to that, having had to hide her own nature."

"Why doesn't she smell like a wolf then?" an older woman asked.

"She was born to rogues but without a wolf inside her," the Alpha said carefully neutral. It was clear he wanted to see how this played out.

There was some laughter, a few shouts asking how that was possible from the pack, but most of the shifters just seemed surprised. Kian spoke up asking anyone if they knew of this happening before.

"A shifter without a wolf? Never! There must

be something wrong with her," another man exclaimed. "Maybe that's why her parents were rogues, they were cast out of their pack!"

Speaking for the first time in her parents defense Emma said "My father was born a rogue, my mother came from a pack. She took off with him when they fell in love since he was not accepted into her pack." The implication was clear; should she be forced to leave, she wanted Kian with her.

Lex stepped up to the base of the steps near Emma and Kian, and said to the pack, "Our Second wouldn't endanger his people, and I give my congratulations to Kian," then turning back toward the couple, "It is nice to see him happy, Emma."

Kayla walked over with a hug for Emma. Kole stepped up too, eyes serious on the pack.

Finally seeing the support some of the pack clapped in welcome, others grumbling, a few outright mad still. The Alpha said, "Today we all shift and run as together as pack. It has been too long."

"Uncle Russ you know she can't shift with us. Is she supposed to wait here on the porch by herself?" Kian asked angrily.

"This would be the problem with her in our pack, she is yours to figure out Kian. You are the one mated to her. You had to realize she would hinder your abilities to stand as Second beside your Alpha. She may go home by herself, or you are welcome to go with her. If so, don't bring her at all next time." Russ said pointedly as he walked past them taking his clothes off. The pack was all undressing quickly too.

"I will just head home then. Have a good run," Kian said turning to leave.

"That's how it is? A Second should run with his Alpha."

"And a mated pair sticks together," Kian said back.

"That would be your choice." And with that the Alpha let the change have him on a rush of power. The big brown wolf with calculating silver eyes exploding out of him. With a dominant growl and snap towards Kian and a dismissive swish of his tail for Emma he ran off towards the woods. Kian and Emma were left with Lex, Kayla and Kole.

"That could have gone better," Emma muttered.

"Could have gone much worse too. Kian could've been banished." Lex shrugged. "Our Alpha only sees black and white, and you're a very big gray area. Don't be surprised if you lose the right to hold a rank though. That growl wasn't for show Deck."

"This isn't right man, she's our fucking people," Kole huffed out.

A long powerful howl rose from deep within the woods. Emma recognized it as Kian's uncle. Still clothed the three people around them groaned in pain. His uncle was going to force a change from them.

"The Alpha demands obedience," Kian explained to Emma.

"But not you?" Emma asked as Kayla, Kole, and Lex headed towards the woods.

"He wasn't calling me," Kian said.

"Or your wolf don't follow him as Alpha anymore," Kole grunted out just before bending over as a man and landing as a wolf. Kole as a wolf was a dark silvered gray with a white chest. Lex and Kayla changed too. With one last look at her brother the cream-colored wolf trotted off into the woods. Kole and Lex seemed unsure whether to go to the pack. The dark silvered gray wolf, Lex with his dark brown fur lightening to tan face, paced back and forth.

Understanding their loyalty to him Kian said to them, "Go. We will figure this out another day."

Her skin tingling from the power of the pack's changes, Emma asked, "Should I be packing?" Brushing his thumb across her cheekbone, Kian shook his head. "You heard your uncle's threat, right? Choose to run with him, or else."

"Yeah, it was damn hard to miss. I don't know what's going to happen, but I couldn't leave you sitting here." Kian leaned down resting his forehead on hers. "You are my priority now Em."

Emma took a deep breath, pulling in all of Kian's comforting essence she could. Nodding her head she stepped back. "Okay, but you have to change sometimes, Kian I don't expect you to never run as a wolf."

Leading her back to his truck Kian took a moment to think before answering. "I love that your first thought is my well-being. I will change later tonight. You mentioned needing to stock up on food. Let's go grocery shopping," Kian added, saying the last part like it was an adventure.

"I can do that myself Kian." Emma laughed.

"Of course, because you are a strong woman who doesn't need a man," he said with a wink. "Maybe I'm not ready for our weekend to be over yet. Tomorrow we both go back to work, and I'm gonna miss the hell out of you. So let me wander the store with you, then help you unpack it all, huh?"

With an argument like that, how could Emma say no?

Without A Wolf

Chapter 8

Over the next few days Emma switched back and forth from being so happy she could walk on clouds, to stomach-knotting worry over Kian's place in the pack. At first she kept trying to convince herself Kian would be better off if she left town, but realistically, there was no way in hell she was leaving him now. While that might have been her plan that first night after Dusty's Roadhouse, Emma knew her limits, and she wasn't strong enough to break both their hearts now. Her new plan was to smile at every single shifter she recognized from the pack meeting. Not many shifters came into the clinic where she worked. Due to their accelerated healing, innate natural grace, and resistance to most diseases. She'd seen them all around town though, while grabbing a sandwich for lunch, or filling up her gas tank. Most of the time they narrowed their gaze, eyes going werewolf bright. Some smiled back hesitantly though. Emma figured that was progress. This town was really beginning to grow on her, and Kian was the miracle she was always afraid to wish for. Every night spent in Kian's arms was worth whatever attitude she had to put up with.

Walking out of work smiling to herself at how much difference a week makes Emma spotted Kayla leaning against a smaller SUV parked by her own car. "Hey Kayla!"

Gripping her up in an exuberant hug Kayla said "I'm kidnapping you for the night. I already told Kian that he's been hoggin' you, and it's time for a girl's night."

"Girls night? That sounds fun, whatdaya got in mind?" Emma said laughing.

"Well first off, let's stop by your place and grab you a bag since you're spending the night at my place. I need a trim, so to start the night off I made us both appointments at the salon Split Ends in town. I'll follow you to your place, you can leave your car there. It's gonna snow, and Kian would kill me if I let you drive that little thing back from my place," Kayla said shoving Emma into her car and shutting the door before quickly hopping into her own ride.

That girl was one big ball of energy, but Emma hadn't had her hair cut in a while, so why not! At home Emma changed into black leggings, a white tank top, and a long gray open fronted cardigan. It looked cute, but she could sleep in it too saving her space in her bag. Grabbing a large paisley patterned tote bag and tossing a pair of scrubs for tomorrow, her makeup bag, toothbrush, and phone charger into it she zipped it closed. Remembering a pillow she headed back out into the small living room Kayla was wandering around in.

"This place came furnished didn't it?" At Emma's nod Kayla continued, "Nothing here has you written on it."

"When you're always just passing through its easier to travel light," Emma said locking up and realizing how cold it must look to Kayla who exuded warmth like sunshine.

Climbing into the burgundy SUV, "Oh, Emma, I didn't mean it to sound so bad. I am glad you're finally here though. My brother has been waiting for a long time for you." At the confused look on Emma's face she went on. "He doesn't realize he was, but I have known for years how lonely he was. Kian just gave up hoping there was a fated mate out there for him, and my brother isn't the kind of man who settles for less."

Thinking about that as they drove toward the salon Emma wondered if anyone else realized how perceptive Kayla really was. The radio was on a pop station, and as the first notes of a catchy song started playing Kayla sang along loudly. After the first verse Emma was laughing and singing with her. Pulling into the strip mall with the salon halfway through the second song they stayed in the car belting it out to each other until it was finished. Kayla said, "My Mom's *human* friend owns this place. She has been cutting my hair my whole life. She doesn't know anything though, so zzzziiipppp."

She mimed zipping her lips. Emma nodded her head that she understood as Kayla pulled open the door and they walked in.

Some salons are relaxing with calming light blue and green decor, geared toward stress relief. That was not this place. The walls were painted vibrant berry pink color. This place was unashamedly fun, made for enjoying being a woman. The kind of place women dished openly with each other about their sex lives, and everyone would ask how many times you got off, or asking how well he was hung. There were women seated in lilac purple chairs laughing with the stylists snipping away at their hair. A comfortable white loveseat next to a coffee table loaded with magazines and books full of hairstyles. Emma immediately loved everything about it.

Before they could even sit down a stylish woman in her fifties with a light blonde bob haircut and square rimmed pink leopard glasses walked over wrapping Kayla up in a hug. "Oh, sweetie, it's so good to see you! Is this the beautiful woman

Hannah was telling me about? Said she got a call from Kian gushing about his new girlfriend! Hi, honey, Emma isn't it? I'm Tess, I can't wait to get my hands in that spectacular hair of yours. It's naturally that color too? Don't ever color it! Women have been coming to me trying to replicate that shade of auburn for years!" Leading them to chairs she asked, "Just a trim Kayla? I love that pixie on you. Makes you look like a woodland sprite."

"Yeah Tess, just a trim. I really love it. Thanks for talking me into it." Turning to Emma she explained, "I used to always wear it really long."

"What about you Emma?" Tess asked as Kayla walked away with the shampoo girl.

"Hhhhhmmm, I haven't had it cut in long time now. What do you think?"

"Nothing too short, or you would be fighting frizz with those curls all the time. Maybe take a few inches off, and add lots of layers to really showcase all the texture, and maybe frame your face," Tess said running her fingers through the weight of

Emma's hair.

"Sounds good to me!"

After getting shampooed, conditioned, and settled back on to one of the purple chairs Emma watched Tess work on Kayla's hair. Taking little snips here and there it was almost magical, like a dance her hands were doing. It was obvious Tess loved her job, and she was very good at it. In no time at all she was running a blow dryer over Kayla's hair, and rubbing a little pomade in her fingers she tousled it just so. "Thanks Tess, now I don't look like a little boy anymore." Kayla laughed.

"Oh, Kayla, you're beautiful. Nothing about you says little boy! And if anyone thinks that they're clearly lacking all common sense," Emma immediately said. Kayla seemed taken aback by the compliment, but Tess wasn't.

"Exactly what she said. It takes a special kind of woman to pull off this look, one with an innate sense of style. And you my dear have it in spades." Giving Kayla a kiss on the cheek, "Come on Emma before your hair is completely dry." With a squeeze on Emma's shoulder she knew was a quiet thanks for what she said to Kayla, Tess got to work.

An hour later they were saying their goodbyes. Emma's hair felt lighter on her head. "Your hair looks like flowing fire now Emma. I love it!" Kayla said as they were leaving. They picked up a pizza from the place a few doors down in the strip mall. "I've got loads of DVD's at home, and I should have enough wine. We should be set." On the drive outside of town Emma texted Kian.

"What are you gonna do without me tonight?"

"Watch a game, drink some beer. Listen to my brother snore. Kayla booted him to my place tonight. Rather have you here. You smell good ;)"

"Tell him to snuggle you if you miss me too much. :P"

"Yeah, right! Have fun babe."

"I already am! We got haircuts......"

"I'm sure I'll be getting a call soon from my mon, then. Knowing Tess, she is already on the

phone with her."

"I liked her, and Kayla said she made my hair look like fire."

Kian sent her a fire emoji, so she sent a kissy face back. Then he said, *"See you tomorrow, miss me."*

"Always," Emma answered as they pulled up at Kayla's house.

Emma recognized it since she passed it on her way to Kian's every time. Kayla had the first house on the private drive Kian lived on. She knew all the pack lived close together, but he hadn't pointed out who lived where. It was a big old farmhouse, two stories, light blue with a large front porch painted white. "The house has been here for over a hundred years. When my grandfather was young he built the private drive and bought up land all around here. That way the pack could buy chunks of it for their own homes. It's where I grew up. Mom left it to Kole and I to share. Kian already had his place by then."

"It's lovely Kayla, I can almost see you three

running around as kids," Emma said. The inside was all done in jewel toned shades with white trim. Rich sapphire blue walls, teal sectional couch, bright yellow throw pillows, wooden coffee table painted a glossy ruby red. The kitchen had white cabinets with a gorgeous shimmering blue granite countertop. It shouldn't have worked, but somehow it did. It was comfortable, and inviting, the kind of place meant for gatherings.

"I like a lot of color. Kole bitches that it's too much, but he doesn't change it."

"This place screams you. I can see why my rental looked so boring to you."

Nodding her head Kayla set the pizza down. "Red or white?"

"Never red," was Emma's immediate response.

Laughing, Kayla got out glasses. "Got it." Wine and pizza in hand they settled on the couch.

Two movies and three bottles of wine later Emma and Kayla swore they would make this a regular thing. Kayla headed up to bed, asking if

Emma wanted to come up to the guest room. Too tired to bother she grabbed one of the blankets tossed on the couch and told Kayla she was good where she was. That way she wouldn't wake her when she got up for work. Feeling thankful she remembered to set her alarm and plug her phone into the charger earlier she drifted off to sleep.

Chapter 9

Starting the shower the next morning Kian shouted for Kole to get his ass out of bed and start the coffee. "It's your damn house," came the muttered response. Knowing once Kole was awake he was up Kian hopped in the shower. Hearing his phone ring while he was mid-shampoo Kian rinsed off quickly. By the time he was out the ringing had stopped. A voicemail dinged as Kian wrapped a towel low around his waist and walked out of his bathroom. Turning it on speaker to listen while he pulled on jeans and a navy-blue thermal Henley for the day.

"Kian, I will be out of state for a few days, I expect you to handle everything while I am gone. Put Kole as foreman at the site, you stick to the office. I'll be letting Cathy know. We can discuss your place in my pack upon my return. I suggest you use this time to evaluate whether this Emma is

worth it." Russ ended the voicemail.

Shaking his head, Kian definitely needed some coffee after the bomb his uncle just dropped into his lap. Gulping down his first cup of scalding coffee before it had the time to cool he fried up a half dozen eggs, and a pound of bacon. Kian was slathering butter on a stack of toast as Kole walked in. Freshly showered himself, his hair was still wet. Kian looked up from the toast, "Whoa, what's got your eyes glowing already?"

Playing his voicemail to Kole, Kian sat down to eat. Putting the food in his mouth and chewing mindlessly. "Holy shit man." Kole loaded his own plate with food.

"I honestly don't get why this pisses him off so much. She is a shifter for chrissakes," Kian said polishing off his first piece of toast.

"A broken one. Guess he doesn't think the next generation of Deckers should come from Emma. Have you considered that your pups might not be able to shift either?"

"That doesn't matter to me Kole. I love her."

"Look, I like her, she seemed to have pulled the stick out of your ass that's been there since Dad died," Kole said. "Maybe Mom can talk to him? But you better get your wolf calmed down because it's making me feel on edge. You don't wanna be picking Emma up like that."

"I'm trying Kole, shit. My wolf is screaming at me to protect my mate." Kian had his hands braced on the counter, the tension rolling through his body. Taking a few deep breaths, making the effort to calm himself one muscle at a time. "Load the dishwasher and clean up will ya? I need to go pick Emma up. Seeing her will help."

"Alright man."

"Keep things going smooth on site. We don't need delays," Kian said as he walked out to his truck.

Gathering up the dishes Kole set about putting the kitchen to rights.

Not bothering to knock Kian used his key to let himself into the house he grew up in. Kayla might have changed the look of the place, jazzing it up with splashes of colors everywhere, but it still felt like home to his heart. Probably always would. Still clad in her pajama's Kayla wandered down the stairs. "Morning big brother. I took good care of your mate last night as promised."

Kissing the top of his sister's head as she hugged his waist. "I knew you would Kay. Your wolf is a real ripper."

She nodded her head. "Damn right she is. Don't forget it."

Emma walked out of the hall bathroom then, and all thoughts drained out of Kian's mind. She was dressed for the day already, dark pink scrubs today. She had on what he noticed was her work makeup, a little mascara on her lashes, and rosy tinted lip balm. Her dark red hair was full of attitude and curling around her face. "I like your hair babe." Kian leaned in for a kiss. Wrapping her arms around him Emma opened her mouth and he rolled his tongue against hers. Rubbing her bottom lip with his thumb Kian added, "Kayla, yours looks real pretty too."

"Such a good man." Emma smiled.

"Thank you. I had a great time last night Emmz," Kayla said putting bagels into the toaster. "Kian already ate, do you like butter or cream cheese on your bagel, I have regular and the strawberry kind."

"Ooooo! Strawberry definitely." Emma smiled.

While the girls ate their breakfast Kian filled them in on his voicemail.

***

The stress of the last week and a half was beginning to take its toll on Kian. Working with Cathy every day was exhausting. She made it very clear multiple times that she wasn't too sure they should welcome Emma into the Big Woods Pack. He knew she purposefully made extra paperwork for him every day. Trying to keep him at the office late so he wasn't able to spend as much time with his mate. Didn't matter, that wouldn't lessen his affection for Emma, but it sure succeeded in pissing him off. He was leaving the office on time today, even if he had to fire Cathy to do it. Hell, he was considering doing that anyway. Cathy could have worked for the FBI as good as she was at gathering information. There is a monumental difference between staying informed about his pack members, and the endless gossip she spread. How his uncle got anything done was beyond him.

As soon as the clock ticked over to five Kian gathered his stuff to leave. Putting power into his words Kian said, "We are done for the day Cathy. It is time to go." Knowing better than to argue with him didn't stop the dirty looks she was aiming his way as she shut her computer down for the day and grabbed her purse. Pulling on her coat she walked out of the office with an exasperated huff. Glad that for once she kept her comments to herself Kane locked the office up and drove home. Knowing Emma would be at his house soon Kian decided he was going to throw some steaks on the grill for dinner. All thoughts of having it ready for Emma when she got there fizzled when he saw Kole's dark blue truck parked in his drive, and his brother pacing in the front yard.

Parking next to his brother's truck Kian stepped out of his. "What's going on Kole?"

"When is Russ coming back? I wasn't cut out to be in charge of the crew. I am so tired every night from all the decisions every single fucking day. I'm not you, that's the perks of being the younger brother. You have to be responsible Kian, but that's never been my thing."

"And I'm not Kole? I've got Cathy buzzing in my ear every day about who got a new car, who's trying for a baby, who might be wearing too much makeup lately, and how she thinks Emma isn't right for our pack. The paperwork is all fucked up, Russ wasn't as on top of it as he should have been. I'm sorry you haven't been able to hunt pussy down in Grand Rapids in a few fucking days. This is the first night I am even going to be able to eat with my mate!" Kian ran his hands through his hair frustratedly as Emma arrived, pulling her car up behind his truck.

"I just want to know when Russ is coming back. You know my wolf is wild. He needs the action for me to keep him in line! Pussy isn't everything to me Kian! Fuck you!" Kole yelled, letting a pissed off growl roll out of his throat his eyes gone a bright silver, and the air was heavy with fur.

"Calm yourself down now Kole!" Kian said low.

Past all reason, a wolf ripped out of Kole. With a look telling Emma to stay in her car, ready for a fight Kian let his wolf have him.

***

Emma watched as a humongous wolf landed on four paws. Kian as a wolf was breathtakingly magnificent. Golden fur darkening to black across his back and ears, bright silver eyes, giant paws. As deadly as he was beautiful Kian launched at his brother. Emma could hear the sound of teeth gnashing together over all the growling. It was obvious that the brothers were both brawlers, and they had fought each other often. Through her mate bond with Kian she could feel his anger at Kole, and his surge of adrenaline coursing through her own veins. The air was crackling with so much dominance Emma had to fight her knees buckling under all the weight pressing against her shoulder blades. Locking her spine, refusing to bend. Emma absolutely would not be weak in front of her mate.

Kian's teeth latched onto Kole's neck and they both stilled. It was clear that Kian could end his brother's life if he wanted. Kian held his brother for a moment waiting to feel Kole comply. The golden wolf backed up a step and shifted into Kian. He watched his brother a moment, then demanded he change back. Kole immediately shifted back into his skin. He was bleeding from claw marks on his thigh, and a bite on his shoulder. His whole chest was darkening with purple bruising. Shaking his head Kole walked naked through the snow towards his truck. Not bothering to cover his swinging dick

Emma arched an eyebrow. Shrugging his shoulders Kole hopped up in his truck and backed out of the drive.

Emma looked back at Kian who was still standing in the yard. There was a cut under his eye, and some bruising down his side.

Her heart was racing, her body felt electrified. "I can feel your wolf. He is pacing inside of you." He narrowed his eyes on her taking a deep breath through his nose. No doubt smelling how turned on she was. His dick rose, hardening as he walked briskly to her. Not slowing his step he bent down picked Emma up by the waist and tossed her over his shoulder. Rubbing his hand up her thigh Kian squeezed her ass hard. It was rougher than he usually was, but she moaned liking this side of him. He carried her through the front door into the house.

Setting her down he leaned in, lips crashing on hers hard. Biting her lip he pushed his tongue into her mouth instead of waiting for her lips to open up. Pressing his dick against her middle Kian backed her up against the wooden door. Emma ran her hands up his chest around his neck into his dark blonde hair. Emma kissed him back, her own tongue dancing with his. He was growling into her mouth, and it broke all the restraint on her control. Emma dug her nails into his scalp. Kian pulled back long and looked down on her with the hungriest look she had ever seen in her life. Emma pulled off her top and unsnapped the front clasp of her bra. Kian licked his lips and reached his hands out grabbing her breasts. Holding them up to his mouth he ducked his head down licking one nipple then the other.

Desperate for more Emma kicked her shoes off, hooked her thumbs in her waistband, and shoved her pants and undies down. As soon as her legs were clear of the pants Kian ran his fingers down her sides all the way past her hips. He let her feel his short nails, but never broke the skin. Emma put her hands on his shoulders as Kian hooked his hands behind her knees and lifted her up. Kian drove his dick deep inside of her. Emma closed her eyes on a quick intake of breath. He felt so damn good.

"Let me know if I get too rough," Kian ground out between clenched teeth, growl constant in his throat.

Knowing exactly how bad he needed her right now Emma buried her head into the side of his neck. His animal scent was stronger here, and she couldn't get enough of his wild smell. Licking and sucking where his shoulder met his neck Emma pulled her knees together holding him closer. Kian was moving in small strokes deep inside pressing against her clit. The pressure was gathering in her middle. Emma leaned her head back against the door. Arms wrapped around his neck she scraped her nails down his back. Emma cried out, her orgasm clenching around his dick.

"Not enough, need more," Kian groaned walking them across to his kitchen table. Setting Emma on her feet he turned her and with a hand pressed against her back pushed her down onto the table. The cold wood felt so good against her skin, making her already sensitive nipples harden. Hands on her hips, Kian pulled her ass up in the air. Rubbing his dick across her clit she moaned. At the sound Kian shoved back into her. He was so deep inside of her with this new angle. Emma sprawled her arms out in front of her on the table and turned her head back to look at him. Kian looked so hot, his eyes were glowing silver bright, lips peeled back, teeth clenched looking down where their bodies collided.

"Harder," she demanded.

"Are you sure Emma?" Kian growled out.

"Yes, harder Kian!" she shouted.

Kian reached up grabbing a handful of her hair pulling it. Forcing her head back. He pumped into her hard over and over again. His balls were swinging up and hitting her clit. Gasping for breath she shoved her ass back into him absorbing his punishing pace. She could feel him getting harder, she was so close when he dug his fingers into her hip. Emma was whimpering now as her legs started shaking. Gasping in air as the orgasm streaked through her, lighting her entire body up. While she pulsed around him Kian's strokes stuttered, his own release filling her. Releasing her hair and laying his head against her back Kian said breathlessly, "I love you Emma."

Still sprawled on top of Kian's kitchen table, her body humming from their lovemaking Emma took a second to let Kian's declaration sink in. She knew they were mates but hearing him say that broke down the last walls she had around her heart. Kian filled up every hollow space inside, chasing away all the shadows made of pain, doubt, and fear. Emma was loved. Nobody had said that to her in 16 long years, not since her Dad left. Taking a deep breath so she could tell him without a shaky voice, Emma replied, "I love you Kian." Hearing his sharp intake of breath Emma smiled. He didn't expect her to say it back, he said it not for a response, but because he needed her to know. Kian's love was a gift, freely given. That made her love him even more.

Kian pulled Emma up, and turning in his

arms she wrapped her arms around his neck. He tightened his arms, holding her tighter. The whole world seemed to hold its breath as their souls melded with that last link in the bond. They loved. Neither one would ever be alone again. Emma would have a family now, and she would give Kian her all for as long as she had. Brushing her hair back from her face Kian had tears in his eyes this time when he said, "Mine."

Nodding her head Emma told Kian, "Nobody but you."

Chapter 10

The world felt brighter to Emma, air tasted a little crisper. It might be cliche but that really was the way being newly in love felt. Emma could actually see the glow coming off her skin, it was as if she was a whole new person molded out of the best components of the old Emma, with none of the darkness. Walking into her rental house Emma took a long look around, and seeing the space with new eyes, she decided right then she needed to add some pizazz to the place. She had been operating on auto pilot for far too long. The house was functional, and clean, but there was nothing welcoming here. Meant to be completely neutral to appeal to everyone, and she had been fine with leaving it that way, before. Now deep in her soul she needed to add some of herself in, make it feel as if she was staying someplace for once, instead of always having one foot out the door leaving. There was nothing here to tell the story of who she was. Leaving a text for Kian that she had some errands to run, but that they were still on for dinner at Dusty's later she ran back out to her car.

Wondering to herself why she hadn't made the trip sooner Emma walked into the store snagging a cart. Since this was a big box store nothing here would be one of a kind unique finds, but she could easily add some color and vivacity to her home. Besides, while she was here, she could pick up some more of her apple scented shampoo and conditioner. Kian was crazy about them, and Emma never wanted to run out. Wandering the aisles with her goal in mind she had her cart filled in no time at all. A bunch of pale gray faux suede pillows to pile on the couch, a soft mint green blanket with fringe, all different frames she planned on putting pictures of her with the people she loved in. There was this cute little bamboo plant in a fat blue pot she had to have, a trio of squat vanilla scented candles to set on a decorative cracked glass plate. Emma also grabbed a half dozen DVD's since she planned on having more girls' nights with Kayla, maybe at her place next time.

Feeling absolutely delighted with all her new purchases Emma was loading them into the back of her little black hatchback when her phone rang. Thinking it must be Kian she answered without ever looking at the screen. "Hey babe!" Emma said with a smile.

"Emma Lowe?" a stranger asked. He sounded much older than her.

Pulling the phone away to see the number was not one she recognized, but wondering if it was maybe a coworker, or member of the Big Woods pack reaching out to her Emma answered, "Yeah, that's me."

"Your father was murdered. He took something from the wrong person, and didn't hide himself well enough. Now you're in danger too. You need to leave Michigan, never look back if ya know what's good for you."

"Who is this? How do you know I am in Michigan?"

"Just someone that doesn't want the same thing happening to you that happened to your old man."

"My father left me, he ran off."

"Patrick Lowe never would have left you girl. You and Beth meant everything to him."

"Who are you? How did you know my father?"

"He may have been rogue, but that doesn't mean he didn't have friends around. Now, like I said, you're in danger, you gotta move on."

"Why me? What have I done to anyone? I can't just leave, I'm mated. His pack is here. He will protect me if you tell me who wants me gone. If you know who killed my father, please just tell me." Emma finally sat down in her car with tears filling her eyes.

"There is so much you don't know Emma. Just watch your back. I can't help you," a deep breath full of regret, "any more than I could help

Patrick."

Emma said, "Then tell me," as the line went dead.

The wave of happiness she had been riding high on crashed. Terrified and confused Emma locked her car door as she raced out of the parking lot. The forest hugging the road had looked so beautiful, almost magically welcoming on the drive up, she had imagined running as a wolf through the trees, the crisp snow-covered ground crunching underneath the pads of her paws. Reminded yet again that she didn't have a wolf, the forest seemed dark and menacing now. Now that Emma could feel Kian's wolf through their bond, she had been imagining herself as a wolf often lately. At least her eyes were still better in the dark than a human's, and she scanned the dark trees constantly for a threat. Breathing a giant sigh of relief at the sight of Kian's truck still at work Emma parked next to him, tossed the car into park and ran into his office on shaking legs. Kian was sitting at his uncle's desk working at the computer. Feeling her inner turmoil as soon as she walked in he was up and wrapping her in his strong arms. Emma let his strength surround her, a feeling of safety blanketing the fear.

"What happened Emma? Are you okay?" Kian growled out, eyes sparking silver blue. Starting at the beginning Emma explained everything, telling her mate about what the mystery caller had said about her family, and how she was in danger. Reaching into the pocket of his dark jeans Kian pulled his phone out. One arm still holding Emma to him he looked through his contacts and put the phone up to his ear.

"Hey Deck man, I'm still at work for a while, can I call you back later?" his good friend Lex asked.

"Lex, can you meet me at my place in a few, something happened, and I need your help," Kian said.

"Okay man, I will be right there. Is Emma alright?"

"She is safe. Upset, but safe." Kian ended the

call.

With Emma in the front seat of his truck, after all her bags were stashed in the back seat Kian sped towards his house. "Can you please text Kayla and Kole? I know you're upset babe, but I need them to come over too. Just say '911, my house immediately'. Okay?" Kian asked handing his phone over. "I will keep you safe, I promise." Eyes burning bright with determination.

Emma nodded her head, and sent the text to both of Kian's siblings with hands still a little shaky, and handed the phone back to Kian. Emma was so lost in her thoughts, her mind racing, trying to remember the last few days with her Dad. Had anything seemed off to her? No, he was the same as he always was. Strict, protective, but so very loving and funny. Maybe something had happened while she was in school that day? He would have wanted to keep her safe. Kicking herself for every time she had gotten mad at him for running out on her. If he was murdered he hadn't left her on purpose, the guilt she felt at not knowing all these years ripping her up inside. Wishing for the millionth time she had a wolf so she wasn't always the weak link, they pulled into Kian's garage. He turned the truck off and shut the door behind them locking them inside the garage.

"I need you to stay here a minute. I have to check my house. Get into the driver's seat. If I'm not back in three minutes, or if you feel something wrong I want you to take this truck and get the hell out of town, okay baby. Just start heading south, call Kayla, tell Kole, he will help you. I trust them absolutely. As my mate everything of mine is yours. If something happens to me it would be enough to set you up somewhere else." Kian kissed her, savoring her mouth a beat before he got out of the truck. She climbed into his vacated seat gripping the steering wheel and hoping that kiss wasn't a goodbye.

Focusing on their bond while watching the clock she felt Kian's anger as he went through the house room by room. He was ready to rip into any threat that came his way. He would enjoy it after everything she told him. But, before the three minutes were up Kian walked back into the garage. "Everything is as it should be in there, the only scents were ours. Come on, they should be pulling in any minute." He grabbed her hand and they walked in.

"I felt your determination to follow my instructions you know. You would have done exactly as I said if I went down, even with your heart breaking. I am in awe of your strength Emma," Kian said kissing the top of her head.

"It's not strength Kian. It would have been disrespectful to your sacrifice to not follow the instructions," she said with a half-smile up at him.

Just as Emma was sitting down on the couch she heard a car pull in. Kian went to the door and checked. "Kole just pulled in with Kayla."

Before they were even in the house Kian said "Lex is here now too. Looks like we'll only have to go over this once."

Kayla was the first in running right to Emma, followed by Kole, then Lex looking very official in his county sheriff uniform. "Emma, are you okay? What's going on Deck? She is as white as a sheet, and I can smell her terror from here," Lex said.

With bright silver eyes, reeking of fur, and filling the air with dominance Kian let everyone know about the phone call. Then he told them all about how she went into the foster care system at twelve thinking her Dad ran off. Kayla held on to her hand the whole time. Kole was pacing back and forth across the living room growling low. Lex stood next to Kian, his brown eyes swirling with silver but with his cop face on, trying to hold his wolf at bay, and taking notes in his little pad of paper.

"Okay, can I see your phone Emma?" Lex said. Before Emma could stand up to hand it to him Kian was there with his hand out for it, moving so fast he almost blurred. "I want to see what I can find out about the caller, hopefully the number leads somewhere. Have you called the Alpha, Kian?"

"Yeah, while I was checking out the house. He didn't answer. I didn't bother leaving a voicemail. He hasn't spoken to me at all since he left two weeks ago. Which is pretty fucking shitty of him. I mean, what kind of an Alpha does that?" Kian said running his hands through his hair messing it up.

"Okay, are we bringing the pack in on this one Kian?" Kayla asked. "They could help protect Emma."

Kole shook his head. "I don't think we should. Nobody's been very supportive of her. And I don't want them to use this as the reason they need to see her as weak and banish her. Then Russ wouldn't even have to."

"I agree with Kole on this one. I overheard some pack rumors that Russ was waiting for you to make a fool out of yourself. That his trip is so he can prove you aren't worthy of Second. We also don't know where the threat originated from, and can't afford to trust anyone but us here with this. At least not until I can find out more information,"

Lex said shaking his head.

"You're right, no pack in this Kayla. I don't know what game Russ is playing, but I am not about to make it easy for him to push me out," Kian said making the final decision.

"I was only thinking strength in numbers. I'm not used to feeling like I can't trust my pack, or my Alpha," Kayla said sadly.

Lex said, "Okay, I am going to take this back to the station. I will let you know what I can come up with."

"In the meantime, Emma shouldn't be left alone at all," Kian said to everyone. With his eyes on her, "Guess you're moving in with me, babe."

Emma nodded.

"I can stay here with her when you're at work, I'm on evenings right now," Kayla said.

"Once I get off shift tonight I have the next two days off. I can come over, check in. I'll let you know what I find," Lex added walking out.

Standing up Kayla said, "I am more than capable of protecting your mate Kian! I would never let anything happen to Emma on my watch." Fists clenched, eyes narrowing, a growl rumbling in her chest.

"You're the one that said strength in numbers Kay. He didn't mean it like that. Lex is trying to help," Kian told his sister who was still fuming. "I know you would keep Emma safe for me. I am trusting the three of you with her life."

"I appreciate this you guys. I'll call and leave a message at work about having to go out of town on a family emergency or something. Kole, can you bring Kayla to grab my car? If I am hiding it should probably be out of sight. I'm gonna start some dinner. I need a few minutes to process everything, so if you plan on eating dinner tonight you're gonna leave me be. K," Emma said tossing her keys to Kole. "That goes for you too mate," Emma said pointedly at Kian before walking into the kitchen.

"What a brave mate I have. I guess I will bring the bags in from my truck then," Kian said, a lopsided grin spreading even though his eyes were still glowing.

Without A Wolf

Chapter 11

The next few days dragged by without anything new on Emma's mystery caller. Kian felt like he was slowly going mad. Of course he knew Lex was working on it, and that Emma was as safe as she could be with his family looking out for her, but there were never any guarantees in life. He had to work, there were deadlines on projects that had to be met. Decker Construction had been around for three generations, and he couldn't let it fail now. Especially since it was starting to feel like it wasn't just temporarily in his hands anymore. Russ had been gone for a few weeks now, and as far as Kian knew hadn't bothered to call anyone. At what point was he supposed to assume the Alpha had left for good? At least Cathy was finally becoming bearable to work with. She was probably figuring out the same thing he was, that Russ might never come back. Kian didn't like the way she nosed into other people's business at all, and he let her know that was not the way things would work anymore.

Tonight the whole family was going to have dinner at his house, hopefully Lex had uncovered some information to share with everyone. Kayla was cooking them some chili with cornbread muffins. Kian had always loved his family, but the way they had banded together to look after his mate meant everything to him. None of them had complained once, which really helped his wolf. Kian had to change every single day lately to cope with the thought of losing his mate. When he was at the office his wolf spent the whole day ripping his insides to shreds. Howling *home to our mate*, over and over again. Being away from her physically right now was one of the hardest things he had ever had to do. Their mate bond was stronger than ever with danger looming over her head. He knew if something should happen he would feel it even if they were at opposite ends of the earth.

As soon as Cathy peeked her head into the

office to let him know she was leaving for the day he was shutting his computer down. Pretending the stress she could feel emanating off of him was all because of the Alpha's absence was difficult. Like all shifters Cathy could sense a lie. Kian was always careful of what he said to her. As new mates it was widely expected that they would have insatiable hunger for each other though, so if she thought he was always eager to leave for the day he hoped she chalked it up to horniness. Kian knew one thing though, if he didn't start getting to the jobsite more often he was going to stagnate in that blasted office. It might work for Russ, but Kian was two decades younger and he needed more physicality than staring at a computer screen all day. Besides in this day and age with the connectivity available, it shouldn't be a problem. Thinking that having another member of the pack come in to help Cathy out while he was on site would work, Kian locked the office up, and engaged the newly installed security system.

Lex was standing in Kian's front yard when

he arrived home. Naturally an open person Lex had trained himself through his years on the force to shutter his expressions. Right now he wasn't doing a very good job at holding his emotions back. Lex's brown eyes were bright silver, glowing in the darkening evening light. Staring off into the trees opposite Kian's home, the tension radiating off him was tangible. Kian's wolf almost tore out of him as soon as he opened the truck door.

"Tamp it down Lex," Kian said. As the Second he held more power over his friend, although he didn't enjoy using it.

"I'm trying Deck. Just frustrated. Hell, just give me a few more minutes."

"What's got you all riled up Lex?"

"Nothing," Lex clipped out.

"Liar. I have too much on my plate right now to figure out what the fuck is up with you. Get your shit together. I have been waiting for a progress report, and patience isn't something I possess in abundance," Kian said his wolf still shredding his insides, as he headed to the house.

Looking back seeing Lex in the same spot was too much for Kian. "NOW!" The order was laced with power that Lex was incapable of ignoring.

Pissed off that he had to pull rank on Lex like that Kian walked straight to his mate who was currently setting his big wood kitchen table and kissed her hard. Emma didn't fight him at all, she just molded herself to him, allowing him to take comfort in her. His wolf finally settling, Kian pulled back to rest his head on top of her dark red hair. Taking a deep breath of the tart apple and tasting the sweet vanilla of her on his lips Kian felt the tension rachet back to a manageable level.

"Missed you today baby. What did you do?" Kian asked as he set her down and took the chair next to her.

"Laundry mostly, oh I had Kole pick up the rest of my stuff from the rental on his way here too. When this stupid danger passes I can move back in there, but I am sick of having half my stuff where I can't get to it, ya know."

"You don't have to do that. I'd like it if you

stayed here. Permanently, with me." Kian gave her a lopsided grin as everyone sat around the table, "How did I get so lucky?"

Emma shook her head and stood up and dished out heaping portions of the fragrant spicy chili into deep bowls. Kayla passed the plate piled high with warm yellow cornbread muffins around.

"Don't you want to move in with me for good Emma?" Kian asked, his voice tinged with fear.

Looking into his eyes as if he was the only person in the room, "No, Kian, oh baby, no, that's not the part that bothered me. I would love to live here with you, forever if you wanted." Now Emma looked away, staring down at her food, "but I'm the one who got lucky Kian. You all wouldn't have to guard me twenty-four seven if I had a wolf like you guys do."

"He would have us all here even if you had a wolf Emmmmmmmmma," Kole said around a mouthful of muffin. The rest of the table nodding their heads in agreement.

Nobody said anything else after that until

after dinner was all gone, everyone having second helpings of the delicious chili. Needing something to do Kian got up to clear the table. While he was loading the dishwasher Kole wet a washcloth and wiped down the counters, stove and table. Lex wandered out and with a back-slap Kian knew was an apology for earlier started some coffee for everyone. Walking back over to the table it hit him anew that these people here were his whole world. The rest of the pack mattered to Kian, and he had always given his all as their Second, but he was positive losing the four people here right now would kill him.

"So, Lex what were you able to find out?" Kian asked after everyone had their cup of coffee.

"Okay, the call was made on a burner cell, as far as I can tell only used that one time. Probably purchased specifically for anonymity. So, unfortunately I won't be able to tell you who the caller was. But I was able to ascertain the phone was purchased from a gas station in northern Georgia. I doubt someone drove from out of state to buy the phone. So I'm thinking maybe the caller lives in the area. You're from there right Emma?"

"I lived there from twelve to eighteen, yeah," she nodded.

"Were any of your foster parents shifters?" Kayla asked.

"No, none of them. I knew better than to say anything about it too. That was my Dad's number one rule," Emma answered.

"What if they don't live in the area, but are only there right now doing some digging?" Kole asked.

"Into her father's disappearance, yeah, that would make sense." Lex nodded.

"What about her father? Were you able to find anything out about what may have happened?" Kian asked Lex.

"There were no bodies found matching Patrick Lowe's description, but from the file on his disappearance it seems the police down there believe he just ran off. Since an adult has the right to do that, they didn't do much looking for him.

But, shit, I'm sorry Emma, there were remains found just across the South Carolina border a few years later. The medical examiner estimated male mid-thirties, dead less than five years, but due to the condition of the body that was about it. That case is still open."

"What is it about that particular body that makes you think it could be Emma's father?" Kayla asked.

"Call it a gut feeling. The body had no clothing on it, had been burned before being buried deep enough to never surface. The only reason it was even found was a new housing development was put in. Everything was done to make sure it wasn't found. Oh, and that development, was miles of deep forest a few years prior."

"Ok, your gut is enough for me Lex. That was probably Emma's father. Why was he killed?" Kian asked, his hands steepled in front of him, elbows resting on the table.

"That's where it got complicated. He didn't leave much of a trail for me to follow back. But I did find a Beth Lowe killed in a single vehicle accident up in Vermont years prior."

"Had to have been bad to kill a shifter like her," Kole added.

With a dirty look in Kole's direction, "It, ah, shit Emma, it was. She went off the road into some trees. Apparently the impact was enough to sever her spine, internally decapitating her. It would have been instant, but she would have known it was coming."

"It's ok Lex, I don't remember her at all. Don't hold back for fear of hurting my feelings. I would really rather be informed than protected," Emma told him.

"Okay. Weather wasn't a factor, and neither was alcohol. Best they could figure is she swerved to avoid something in the road, an animal probably. But to me, looking at the pictures in the file it looked like there was a car behind her. The back drivers side corner of the vehicle was dented. The investigators who handled it noted that was probably from a nearby tree as the car flew off the road. There was also a skid mark heading away from the scene. The report said the skid mark was probably there prior to the accident and unrelated."

"But..." Kian prodded.

"But to me, it looks like she was run off the road. That is the way I would have called it had I been first on the scene. And that patch of burnt rubber on the road, I would bet my badge whoever ran her off the road sped off to avoid being spotted," Lex finished.

"So, we have two dead parents. One run off a road in Vermont, the other buried in a former forest just over the Georgia/South Carolina border. How many states in between, Emma?" Kole asked.

"I didn't even know about Vermont. I know I started Kindergarten in southern California. We headed a bit north every year or so until I was eight. That's when we moved clear out to Texas. Dad homeschooled me there for two years. We headed over towards Georgia slowly from ten until I was twelve. That's when he put me back in public school. When I asked him why he said it was where a young woman needed to be," Emma said remembering. "That's how it is with rogues though, they have to move around a lot."

"Shit baby. You never had a home did you?" Kian said laying his hand on her thigh under the table. "Rogues just don't belong to a pack. Most of them aren't that nomadic."

"Unless they're running from something. And it seems like her dad was running big time. From what though?" Kayla asked.

"I think I know," Lex said standing up walking to the French doors looking out into the dark woods in the back. "Again, there was no maiden name on record, but the picture of your mother's on her driver's license in the file looked familiar to me. You said your mom was from a pack up north?"

"Yeah, but that's all I know. My Dad didn't talk about her much."

"It was probably too painful. Losing a mate is devastating to our kind. He would have felt the moment of her death. My Mom told me it's hard to recover when half of you feels like it's always missing after that," Kian said referring to his own father's death.

Still staring outside, Lex said into the glass, "I am pretty sure she was my father's little sister MaryBeth. She ran away with her mate at eighteen. They got letters from her for the first year. She was blissfully in love with her new mate. My family was happy for her. I know why she left, but it's going to piss all of you off."

"That would make you my cousin! I've never had a cousin before," Emma said walking over to him and hugging him.

"You have her hair. She had wild dark red hair too. But her eyes were brown. You must get those golden green ones from your Dad," Lex said holding onto Emma.

"I do. He always said he gave me his eyes, but everything else came from his Beth."

Seeing his mate hug another man and crying into his chest wasn't easy for Kian's wolf. But he knew she needed to make that connection to a family she hadn't known she had. Slightly awed by the fact that his best friend in the world and his mate came from the same family tree. Kian smiled a moment for all the happiness those two people brought into his life. Lex had been his friend since he could remember, he held him up when he was drowning after the loss of his father. And Emma was the other half of his soul. It made strange sense that the two people who were so connected to his heart somehow be related. Now that he knew they were family he could almost see a resemblance. Remembering that Lex said he had more information that he wasn't going to like he cleared his throat loudly ruining the happy moment and asked, "And the rest? What is going to piss us off?"

Pushing Emma gently away from him, needing the distance, Lex said, "Another member of the pack always wanted my Aunt MaryBeth, said she was going to be his someday. She never felt the same though, and in the note she left explaining why she had to go, she said she knew he wasn't going to accept seeing her mated to another man. It would be best for her to leave." Both hands in his hair looking at Kian like he was going to lose him for saying this he finished it. "That man was your uncle Russ. You've seen how much he doesn't like me, right? He was always the same with my old man too. Treats us like we are second class pack members. That's why. Shit, I'm sorry Deck, I should have put it together sooner, and I didn't."

Standing up so fast that his chair crashed onto the floor Kian roared, "ARE YOU SAYING MY UNCLE KILLED MY MATE'S PARENTS AND NOW HE WANTS TO KILL HER?"

Not waiting for an answer, Kian stormed out the front door, his wolf ripping out of him as soon as his feet touched the snowy yard. With one last look at the people gathered in his home the dark golden wolf with the black back and ears ran off into the forest.

Chapter 12

A long, agonized howl burst through the air a few minutes after Kian's wolf raced off into the night. Emma was up heading out the door as the haunting notes faded. With a hand on her arm and a shake of his head Kole stopped her. He was probably right, Kian needed to deal. It wasn't as if Emma could shift to follow him, and the last thing he needed right now was his mate wandering into the dark forest after him. There was also still a threat against her life that she had momentarily forgotten. Kian would never forgive her if she were to put herself in danger like that. Covering Kole's hand on her arm with her own she gave it a squeeze to thank him for his wisdom.

Not ready to face the harsh light Lex shed on her history Emma muttered she needed a shower and walked up stairs to the room she was sharing with Kian. His master bathroom was made for unwinding from stress, and Emma wished she could hide out in there all night. With a look of longing towards the large bathtub she walked past to the shower in the corner. It was all stone tile with a glass door. Not surprisingly, modesty was not the main priority when Kian built it, he hadn't gone for frosted glass. Nudity was more accepted with shifters than in human society. Reaching in and turning the water on so it could warm up first, Emma walked over to the counter. Staring at herself in the mirror Emma let herself remember the picture of her mom that she had stared at so many times growing up. She looked so much like her. Aside from her eyes the rest was mostly the same. Wondering if that had anything to do with why another Decker man had fallen for that face. Shaking her head hoping to rid herself of all the doubts swirling inside of it, Emma stripped her clothes off and set them neatly into the hamper in the corner.

The water was steaming hot when she stepped into the stream. Emma let it run over her head, the first of her tears mingling with it. Unable to hold the tide back any longer she sank down in the corner bringing her knees up against her chest, and sobbed. Murdered. Both of her parents had been murdered. Her Mom hadn't died in some accident of fate, she was forced off that damn road in Vermont, right into the trees. Deep down Emma knew even if the impact hadn't been enough she would have died that night. What was going through her head as she swerved off the road? Was it blinding terror? Was it sadness that she wasn't going to get longer on this earth? Was she grateful that Emma and her Dad weren't there with her? Knowing there was never going to be an answer to that stole the air from her lungs.

How had her Dad died? Did Emma even want to know? Was he fighting as a wolf? Shot? It hurt too much to imagine. He must have known the end was closing in, since she had been sent to public school, so her Dad knew she was surrounded by people all day long. It's exactly what she would've done in his position. Patrick brought the picture of his Beth along that day. Having her with him one last time. Knowing she would never see that picture again was just another blow. That bastard had stolen both of her parents from her, and he hadn't even left a picture behind to remember them by. And for what? Because he wanted a woman who never wanted him back? She loved someone else, her fated mate. He never would have been that for her Mom. Never. That simply wasn't the way it worked for shifters. So why the hell couldn't he let go? Was he jealous someone else got to love Beth, or was it that he was angry she chose Patrick over him? How fucking childish of him. Like a naughty little boy who destroyed his favorite toy when he outgrew it so nobody else would ever know the joy of playing with it. All the lives that man ruined. Vowing one way or another Russell wasn't going to win this. He wouldn't get away with taking her parents from her, and she damn sure wasn't going to add herself to the list of his victims.

Finally spent Emma stood up turning her

face into the spray erasing the salty tracks of her tears. Needing normalcy she went through the motions. Washing her hair with the pearly white shampoo. Breathing in the comforting scent of apples as she slicked the thick conditioner onto the lengths, careful as always to avoid bringing it up too close to her scalp. Nobody wanted to get out of the shower with roots already feeling oily. Picking up her razor to shave while the conditioner sat on her hair working its frizz reducing magic. Skin smooth and hairless she lathered herself up with the thick moisturizing body wash.

Emma rinsed her hair and body knowing that when she stepped out of the shower she wasn't going to be the same person that walked into the bathroom an hour before. Her life was smashed to pieces again, but it just wasn't in Emma to stay broken. Pulling on a pair of purple cropped sweatpants and a gray t-shirt she squared her shoulders and walked out. She would always feel the scars lining her soul. Like that cracked plate she bought to hold the candles the other day.

Determined that this was going to make her stronger, because she knew deep down that Russell Decker thought her weak, easily dealt with. Without a wolf she might be, but that didn't mean she would cower for a bully.

Chapter 13

Seated on the couch staring dejectedly into the fire blazing away in the hearth, Lex was the only one left as Emma padded barefoot down the stairs. Giving him space she settled on the opposite end of the sectional, tucking her feet up underneath her. She could feel the uncertainty radiating off Lex in waves. He wasn't sure he was welcome here anymore. "Lex, you know that none of this was your fault right? I am incredibly grateful that you told me. It wasn't exactly easy to hear, but that's not on you. It takes a lot of heart to tell people things you know are going to hurt them. Kian is lucky to have you in his life, and I am too. Nobody's gonna blame you."

"Deck might. His family killed yours. Yeah, that's some soap opera shit Emma." Lex shook his head. Emma wondered to herself what it would have been like to grow up together, as cousins.

"No, not his family. An evil man killed my family. The rest of the Decker's are good, down to their bones good, which is why they didn't know. He hid his true nature from everyone."

"You actually mean that." Lex finally looked over at her. "I haven't told my parents yet. I just couldn't. I'll have to someday though. They were both close with MaryBeth. I can hold them off for a while, but they're going to want to meet you. Dad especially. You look so much like your Mom, that's gonna make him real happy. I've always thought he blamed himself for not leaving with his sister."

Not really sure what to think of that Emma nodded. "I can understand that, I would want to meet me too if I were them. But, won't they be disappointed that I don't have a wolf? That's not exactly something worth bragging about at family reunions."

With a laugh Lex shook his head. "But that doesn't mean we would be ashamed of you. It would just be one thing about you. That's not your whole story Emma."

"Yeah, I guess. Does that run in your family?"

"Our family...." Lex said, his brown eyes warming.

"Our family," Emma murmured with a surprised smile, warmth flooding her at the words that she had never said before.

Seeming happy that she understood Lex said, "Not that I know of. Do you have stronger senses like we do? Can you heal well?"

"Yeah, I heal just like the rest of you do. I have good senses, better than humans, but I'm not sure if they're as good as yours."

"Mine is better as a wolf, but still really good as a man," he replied.

Looking around the house, "When did they leave? It was pretty rude of me to leave everyone down here like that."

"Nah, no worries. They left right after the shower turned on." He hesitated.

"I can hear the half-truth there. I got that handy ability too, Lex."

"Of course you did. They, ah, shit Emma, we heard you break up there. It was rough hearing that knowing there wasn't anything to do to fix it for you. Kayla started to go up to you, and Kole had to stop her. He said you needed to get it all out before you could deal with it. She was crying, so I told them I would stay until Deck gets home. Since this is all on me."

"Oh." If it was one of them up there bawling like that she would have had a hard time listening too. "Wasn't thinking about shifter hearing."

They sat there in silence for a while. Too much had happened, there was too much to say, but words didn't seem to be enough. The only sound the wind moving through trees. Leafless branches creaking. Thinking her stuff looked good scattered around Kian's house Emma wondered if he would still want her as a mate. Lex was no doubt hoping he hadn't lost his best friend. And Kian, her love was running through the night trying to burn the hurt out of himself. She could feel him pushing himself, trying to find relief. It occurred to her that if she was still feeling him then he had felt all her tears in the shower. It would have been nice to spare him that. Wishing she could take Russell Decker down herself right now for making Kian feel her pain she asked Lex, "Do you think I could be turned? Like with a bite? Would that give me a wolf?"

"Hell, I don't know, it could kill you Emma. Even if it didn't, it might not give you a wolf. You were born to shifters, maybe that would cancel it out or something." Lex looked really worried.

"Don't worry I'm not asking you to do it. I was just wondering, is all."

"If Deck wasn't already pissed off at me, that would definitely do it. Changing someone else's mate is one hell of a big no-no." Lex said visibly relieved that she didn't want him to try and turn her.

Emma figured they could both use a distraction. She asked Lex to tell her about his childhood. What it had been like for him growing up. He thought about it for a moment, like he wasn't quite sure where would be a good place to start. He told her how humid the summers in Michigan got, that the air was so thick with moisture it could almost choke you sometimes. So his family and Kian's brought all the kids to Lake Michigan to cool off every chance they got. That people called it the 'big lake' around here since you were never more than six miles from a lake. They would trek across what felt like miles of scorchingly hot sand to pick the perfect spot to set up their blanket. Everyone would be loaded down with coolers full of sandwiches and cans of 'red pop.' Or beach bags filled with toys, towels, a few bottles of sunscreen, and a half dozen bags of chips. When they were really little they would build giant sandcastles with moats dug deep and filled with buckets of water. Once they had buried Kian's Dad and made him look like a mermaid.

Then when they were teenagers and could drive themselves they would go in search of girls. Couple of scrawny sixteen-year olds, tall but not quite filled out yet. Kole sometimes convincing them he should tag along even though he was two years younger. One time they walked down the pier and jumped off the end, even though you really weren't supposed to. They figured since they were badass shifters and all it was no big deal. That rip current was pretty intense though, and it was harder than they thought to swim into shore.

Emma could see the three of them swimming for all they had. Taking more than they planned, battling the churning waters. Apparently youth held bad decisions and teenage stupidity for shifters too. Laughing hard at how they had probably looked like half drown cats when they reached the shore. Emma told Lex she would have liked to see that. Shaking his head he said it hadn't impressed any of the girls, and they all drove home feeling sore and thoroughly water logged. When the laughter died down, they looked at each other smiling.

Chapter 14

It had been one hell of a night. Kian was still fighting the rage and pain swirling inside of him. But he was finally able to gain enough control to shift back. His wolf needed to run the hurt out since he couldn't rip into his uncle yet. He was more determined to put an end to all of this with each beat of his paws on the ground. How would he ever be able to erase all the damage his uncle had caused?

Kian checked on his siblings before heading home. Kayla was in bed, tossing and turning, probably feeling completely helpless to fix everything. Kole was down in the living room feet up on the glossy red coffee table bottle of whiskey half gone, it wasn't easy for their kind to get drunk. With their metabolisms they processed the alcohol too quickly, so they had to drink a whole lot rather fast to get sloshed like humans. But Kole was just trying to take the edge off. Numb the pain a little. Knowing Kian's wolf was outside checking in he raised the bottle in a silent toast before taking another swallow.

He would never have even known about all the evil things his uncle had done if he hadn't met his Emma. With another reason to be grateful for her in his life he walked up the front steps to his porch. Hearing his oldest friend in the world laughing with his mate eased his soul a little. They were finding a way past the pain together, like family was supposed to. Let this be the good that came out of all the shit stirred up tonight. Emma had a family she never even knew about. Kian knew exactly how great it was to have Lex. He would do anything in the world for the people he loved, and Emma was one of his people now.

Lex was telling her about the time their dumbasses had jumped from the end of the pier. He left out that nobody was supposed to go into the water that day. There had been red flag signs posted all over the beach. Or that the current along the structure dragged people out further from shore. Lake Michigan was the deadliest of all the Great Lakes, and she had taken them down a peg that day. The cocksure shifter boys who thought themselves invincible. Letting them have their moment he stood there buck naked on his porch in awe of the way fate worked.

When their laughter quieted, he walked in. Emma immediately jumped up and ran into his arms. Wrapping his arms around her rocking them back and forth a bit. This wasn't going to ruin what they found in each other. Neither one of them would let it. Words weren't necessary, Emma didn't have to tell him her feelings hadn't changed, he could feel her love weaving around him through the bond. Taking a breath, he nodded his head. Kian was going to fix this, avenge his mate's parents. If there was evil in his family, his pack it was on him to eradicate it.

Lex got up from his spot on the couch to leave. Head down, eyes on the floor. That was not right. Still holding onto Emma he reached out, laying a hand on his friend's shoulder. "Lex, shit, I didn't handle that well. It's not on you though, man. You're my best friend, my brother. Thank you for telling us, and for helping my mate when I didn't."

Raising her head to look into his eyes, "Kian, we both needed space to absorb that blow. I felt you the whole time, you didn't really leave me," Emma said reaching a hand out to Lex linking the three of them. "You have always been his, now you're mine too."

"Okay." Giving Emma's hand a squeeze, "I don't know what is going to happen next, but I've got your back Deck. It fucking killed me to tell you."

"I know man. We need to figure out where the bastard is hiding," Kian said.

"I'm all over that. I will know as soon as that piece of shit moves," Lex said, his voice gone cold. "I should go, my shift starts soon."

Lex walked out of the house as the sky was lightening toward dawn. Kian turned toward Emma, she was his whole world. But just being in his life had put her in danger. He knew that made him selfish, but every man had his limit. Her golden green eyes were rimmed red and puffy from crying, but he had never seen anyone more beautiful. Cupping the back of her neck he leaned down and rested his forehead on hers. "Nobody but you."

"Nobody but you, Kian."

Chapter 15

Kian's forehead still resting on hers, Emma knew he wasn't going to like what she had to say. But it needed to be said none the less. "I need your bite. We have to try and turn me."

Pulling away from her far enough to stare into her eyes Kian shook his head. "We can't. There are no guarantees it will work. And I'm not going to do something that could kill you."

Getting frustrated with him, "I was born a shifter. Your bite won't kill me. I just know it won't."

Kian didn't say anything. Just walked up the stairs. Emma got distracted a moment at the sight of her beautiful mate. There was nothing hiding his deliciously sculpted muscles. Emma had the sudden urge to sink her teeth into the globe of one perfect ass cheek. Her man really was hot, like on a scale of one to ten he was at least a twelve. The fact that he didn't seem to notice his beauty only made it more appealing. Reminding her hormones to chill, she strode with stubborn purpose up after him.

"Kian! Don't walk away from me! I'm serious. You need to bite me."

Closing the bathroom door on her he said, "Nope."

Emma crossed her arms at the sound of the shower turning on. It would be easier if she could just bite him and turn. That wouldn't work though. It would just bleed him. She understood why he didn't want to. It wasn't about not wanting to give her a wolf. It was that not everyone survived the turn. He was scared. Once he bit her there was nothing he could do if it started going wrong. That was probably why her parents hadn't done it when they figured out she didn't have a wolf inside. They had wanted her alive more than they needed her to be like them.

Kian walked back out of the bathroom, a white towel wrapped around him, hanging low on his waist. Water still running down from his dark blonde hair. "I won't be able to keep myself safe without your bite Kian. Please don't leave me so vulnerable. Your uncle is going to come for me. We can't keep me hidden here forever. Eventually I have to go back to work. I can help you guys."

Dropping the towel and opening the dresser drawer Kian said, "I love you Emma. More than anything else in this world. Even if I bit you, and it didn't immediately kill you, and you got your wolf, that doesn't mean the danger passes. He got to both of your parents, Emma, and they had wolves. Clearly my uncle has no fucking honor. That isn't our way. We don't kill in this form. We fight our battles as wolves. If that's what he wanted then maybe, just maybe I could get over the risk. But a wolf won't stop him from cutting your break lines, or from putting a bullet into your head as you walk down the damn street."

"You're right. He won't fight fair. But he expects this. He doesn't think you will turn me. So by not biting me you play right into his hands,"

Emma said running her hands up Kian's back. "I don't want to die Kian. I want to raise babies with you, grow old together. On my death bed I want to look back on decades of happiness with you." Feeling him start to tremble and shutter Emma went on. "I really think I need a wolf to make that happen. It doesn't have to be right now, think about it, please just think about it."

"Ok Emma. I will think about it," Kian whispered sounding like a man crushed by the weight of the world.

"That's all I ask." Emma kissed between his shoulder blades, and as Kian turned toward her she kissed along his ribs and over his heart. "I need something good Kian. To drown out all of the pain tonight." Licking a swirl around his flat nipple she closed the drawer he still hadn't taken any clothes out of. She smiled up at him before leaving biting kisses down his abs until she was kneeling. Running her hands up his chest, dragging her nails back down. His dick stood hard and eager in front of her. Unable to resist a moment longer Emma ran her tongue across the broad head. Hearing his sharp intake of breath Emma wrapped her hand around the base, stroking slowly up she licked his head again once before opening her mouth. Taking Kian's dick into her mouth until he hit the back of her throat. Wrapping her lips tight, she sucked as if she was going to swallow him whole.   He growled and his hands gripped her head, as if holding onto her was the only thing keeping him upright. Easing back off him she stroked her tongue back and forth, pressing him against the roof of her mouth. Pulling one hand off his dick she cupped his balls and squeezed gently. The answering grunt was accompanied by a thump of his dick. Feeling powerful Emma picked up the pace. When Kian was grunting breathlessly, she paused, shook her head back and forth. Gripping the base of his dick, Emma twisted back and forth as she worked her head up and down.

"Emma, wait, wait. I'm gonna come," Kian chanted above her. He was getting close. When he went to pull her head off, she grabbed his wrists and held them at his side. Moving her head up and down faster now she felt him twitch, his dick swelling impossibly bigger. He was groaning now with each gasping breath. Then his whole body went rigid a second before he shouted out, and hot spurts hit the back of her throat. Swallowing it all she sucked gently until his body relaxed.

Using her grip on his arms she pulled herself back up. As soon as she was standing his mouth crashed against hers. Shaking hands pulled her t-shirt up, and he broke the kiss only long enough to get it off her head. His mouth still on hers, his tongue stroking in and out of her mouth like his dick just was. He pushed her sweats off her hips leaving her in only cotton panties. Kissing down her neck Kian lifted her up with an arm under her knees. Tossing an arm over his shoulder Emma giggled.

"My turn now mate," Kian said with fierceness. Striding over to the bed with her he set her down gently. "Soaked your panties blowing me didn't you babe," Kian said running a finger across her panties right over her seam. "That was seriously the best head I have ever gotten. Knowing that it turned you on only makes it even better."

Kian sucked on her hip bone, hands stroking up her sides. Emma's nerves were zinging already, and he had barely touched her. Palming her breasts, squeezing them before running his hands back down to open her legs further. Slipping a finger into the side of her panties Kian dipped it shallowly inside of her. Back arching, hips thrusting forward to take more of him in. He pulled it back out, denying her the depth she craved.

Tossing one arm up over her middle pressing her into the bed. "Not yet Emma," Kian said biting her thigh lightly. Blowing hot air onto the cotton covering her clit, his finger back in her panties Kian ran it around her opening dipping barely in. Caught between enjoying the added friction and feeling restricted by her panties Emma moaned. Kian's teeth latched onto her clit, biting gently down as his finger finally went deeper inside her. Growling Kian ripped her panties clear off her.

Guess he was teasing himself too.

With no more barrier blocking her from him Kian leaned in and licked her clit quickly back and forth. She could feel his beard scraping against her most sensitive areas. Turning his hand Kian pushed in all the way, and wiggling the tip of his finger found her G spot. Gripping the comforter in her hands, Emma was gasping for breath, her body shaking with every flick of his finger. Adding a second finger to the first one Kian pulled her clit into his mouth and sucked. Her vision was closing in, everything in her focused on what he was doing between her legs. "Yes, yes, yes," she hitched brokenly. Her orgasm ripped through her, blinding her with its power. When she came back down from the clouds Kian was smiling up at her.

"Holy shit you almost drowned me," he laughed.

"Mmmmmm you're just really good at that." She smiled. "Come here mate."

She pulled him up her body. Settling on top of her Kian kissed the top of her shoulder and eased his dick into Emma. After the orgasms they both just had he was in no rush. He set a devastatingly slow pace. Kian rested his weight on one elbow, the other hand wrapping around the back of her neck holding her while he kissed her. Her hands on his ass, feeling it flex as he moved inside her. He felt so good sliding in and out, filling her completely. His body rubbing against her clit. Feeling the pressure building again her nails digging in. She could feel him closing in too, his kiss turning desperate. Gasping for breath, hips crashing together. At the first pulse of her orgasm she felt him jerk and flood her with his hot wet heat. Kian rocked until all of her aftershocks had subsided.

"Let's sleep for a few hours ok, baby?" he asked. At her nod he pulled the covers down and settled them underneath them. Holding on to each other they drifted off to sleep, leaving the world and all of its problems outside."

Chapter 16

The phone buzzing woke Kian up a few short hours later. Extricating himself as carefully as possible from Emma's arms he checked it as he padded out of the room. It was an email notification. Knowing the world didn't care what was going on in his life, he might as well get started on some business. He put on a pair of faded jeans with holes at the knees, and a dark green long sleeve thermal. Emma was still sleeping peacefully, and knowing she could definitely use it he closed the door on his back out of the bedroom. She was holding it together, but he knew the stress was taking its toll on his mate. He didn't like to work from his phone, so he set his laptop on the bar and logged into his email account. There were a few from suppliers about lumber, tile, and drywall. One from a potential customer requesting an estimate. A bunch of other junk that hadn't gotten filtered into his spam folder, and one from his uncle. No subject. Wolf inside growling, hackles raised, he opened the email.

By now you must have figured out why I left. I retained a lawyer in Grand Rapids to handle my affairs under your name. My share of the company has been transferred to you, my house listed for sale. Think you can take my place as Alpha, you have no idea what I am capable of. By this afternoon the whole pack will know.

Russell Decker

The time stamp said it was sent three hours ago. Running his hands down his face wondering how the hell he was even related to that snake of a man he called Cathy Wyles, the secretary. She would be able to gather everyone quickly.

"I need you to call an emergency pack meeting, my house one hour from now." As soon as Kian hung up, he was already dialing. His brother muttered a greeting into the phone, not bothering to say hi Kian told him to call Lex and Kayla, and get the three of them over to his place immediately. As he hung up his phone the text from Cathy for the whole pack came through.

Mandatory emergency pack meeting at the 2nd's house 1 hour.

Wishing like hell he didn't have to wake his mate up, Kian shook her shoulder gently. "Baby, you're gonna need to get up." Emma blinked sleepily at him once, and sensing the tension rolling off him, sat straight up. So much for letting her sleep. Damn his fucking uncle. Hearing the others pull up he walked back downstairs.

Kole and Kayla came rushing in. "We got the text, what the fuck is going on?" his brother demanded.

"See for yourself," Kian said jerking his head in the direction of his computer on the counter. Kole and Kayla each read it and Kole immediately started pacing.

"Shit, Kian, do you know what that means? He screwed us! He made it look like you ran him out of town! The pack is already upset with you, they're not going to let you take his place as Alpha. This is going to be a bloodbath!" Kole swore pacing back and forth.

"Way to be positive Kole," Kayla admonished him.

Lex walked in and having heard the end of Kole's rant went right over to where Emma was standing at the counter reading the email.

"What does this mean for the rest of us?"

Emma asked.

"I need to establish myself as the new Alpha," Kian said, his eyes bright.

"I know you're the Second, it should be easy right? Please tell me it will be easy for you," Emma said hopefully looking at him. Kian didn't answer Emma.

Not wanting to lie to his mate, but knowing she wouldn't like the answer. He just shook his head.

"Kian fought off challengers for his rank occasionally, and he is dominant enough. But Kole is right. Kian isn't very popular at the moment. That was a damn good powerplay, he didn't give us the opportunity to do any damage control," Lex said, then kneeling, "We are going to have to fight. I am with you Deck, I've had your back since we were pups. I pledge my fealty to you, by tooth and by claw, you are the Alpha."

Kole and Kayla joined Lex on his knees, pledging themselves to Kian as well. Emma stood there, not knowing what to do since she didn't have a wolf, and wasn't an official member of the pack. Kayla grabbed Emma's hand and pulled her down next to the others.

Kian accepted their submission under him with a feral growl. "I will be honored to be your Alpha. I don't want my first act of leadership to be asking you to fight friends and neighbors today, but that's what is coming our way. But we will not go down easily." He looked at his mate, her question to him clear in her eyes. Shaking his head no, he wouldn't bite her. Knowing he couldn't focus on the task at hand while worrying over her first turn, if she was lucky enough to survive it. She sighed, and that sound of disappointed defeat shot straight into his heart, cracking it a little. He knew it was hurting her to be denied. "That won't help now. After this has all been settled we will look for other answers. There has to be information somewhere, maybe your father couldn't figure it out while on the run hiding you."

Emma nodded her head, and he knew she didn't believe that was the case. But she didn't press the matter.

Chapter 17

The next hour was spent pacing, and being really pissed off at the selfish, childish actions of a small-minded man. Emma could tell Kian was trying to remain hopeful that this would all work out in their favor without bloodshed. As for her, she just wanted this over. Without having the power to shift she wouldn't be much use if the pack didn't accept Kian as Alpha. They would be stupid not to though, he was a good man, the best. He would be a far better Alpha than his uncle ever was, but change was never easy. Some people always fought it, swimming against the tides. The truth was on their side, but the loyalty to Russell Decker ran deep.

Kian tried to convince her to wait inside, but everyone had agreed it set a bad precedent. For Emma to be part of the pack, they had to let her stand with them. He didn't like putting her in danger like that, but he knew they were right. If he didn't think she was strong enough to belong then nobody else would either. Determined to be strong Emma tucked her fear deep inside.

Emma shoved her feet into snow boots, but didn't bother putting a coat on. Her jeans and purple sweater would be warm enough. She had always run a little warmer, and since their mated bond was strong now, the residual energy from Kian's wolf provided her with even more warmth. Joining Kian and the others on the back porch Emma could hear the vehicles approaching. There were a lot of them, but they didn't seem to be racing in. She took that as a good sign. As the first people came around the back Kian stepped forward, and slightly in front of Emma. Ever the protective mate.

When everyone was gathered in the back yard Cathy Wyles stepped forward, "I received a phone call from a law office just after you asked me to set up a pack meeting. I was told the three of you are the sole owners of Decker Construction, and that you, Kian, hold the deed to your uncle's house."

"That's bullshit!" Kole said.

Kian held a hand up to silence him.

Cathy's mate Gerald Wyles said, "What did you do son?"

Kian said, "My Uncle, the former Alpha of the Big Woods Pack is a coward. He ran away weeks ago. He made it look like I stole the business, and his house. He is manipulating everyone because I learned the truth of who he is." At the uproar from the crowd Kian paused, waiting for them to quiet. "He ran because evidence came to light that he murdered a pack member, and her mate."

"Lies!" Cathy shouted.

"You can't know he did that!" someone else said.

Looking over at Lex Kian said, "He can."

Lex stepped forward, "Emma received a phone call telling her that her parents were murdered and warning her that she was going to be the next target. Kian asked me to look into the threat. I traced the call to northern Georgia, where Emma lived when her father disappeared. A few years after his disappearance some male remains were found matching her father's description just over the border into South Carolina. Using the information in Patrick Lowe's file, I found the accident report from his wife's death a decade prior. Beth Lowe's car was forced off a road in Vermont into some trees. Coroner's report stated she died on impact. Beth Lowe was MaryBeth Kolter. My father's younger sister, and Emma's mother."

Kayla stepped forward, "See! She has every right to be a pack member. She comes from this pack!"

"I liked MaryBeth, I can see that Emma looks like her, but why would Russ have hunted her down? She broke no laws leaving with her rogue," Cathy growled at them. "He wasn't even the Alpha back then. Your grandfather was."

"Because my uncle thought himself in love with MaryBeth, and if he couldn't be the one to have her, then nobody would. She was not his mate, did not feel the same for him. Patrick Lowe was her true mate. She wrote letters to her family of how happy they were, and how wonderful it was to be mated," Kian said. He knew the pack didn't believe him.

"Your mate started all this! It's all her fault!" an old man said angrily.

"How? Russ would have done those things years before Emma showed up in town. It sounds like Kian is telling the truth," Jase, a pack member who worked the construction crew said coming to their defense.

"These four standing here have already pledged fealty to me as their Alpha," Kian growled. "This is my pack now."

"Russ isn't here to defend himself from these claims. They ran him off because Kian couldn't fight him in a true Alpha challenge. Her showing up caused this." The old man pointed at Emma. "It was all in the past, long forgotten. Your pack? Funny you should mention that. The Alpha called me to tell me that you three had worked the law to steal the business out from under him, because he didn't want to make your girl a member of your pack you all chased him out of town. That he barely escaped with his life. I didn't want to believe that of you boy, but he said you had shown your true colors, and I think he was right." A snarling gray wolf ripped out of the old man.

Kian let out a yell that ended in a howl. This was it. There would be no more talking. Everyone was shifting now. Lex's big brown wolf, and Kole's dark gray and silver wolf flanked Kian's golden wolf on either side. Even Kayla shifted and ran into the action. Emma watched the pack tear into each other. A solid black wolf ripped a smaller tan one off Kian. Not everyone believed in Russ it seemed. It looked like five against fifteen now, the odds still stacked against them. Pissed off that there was nothing she could do to help she noticed a mottled gray wolf slipping away from the action heading her way. As soon as the wolf's eyes locked on hers she knew it was coming to end her. Emma looked for Kian one last time.

Instead she saw Kayla's cream wolf racing towards her. Hoping Kayla made it before the other wolf Emma backed against the house. Kayla barreled into the gray wolf's side, knocking it off its deadly trajectory. Planting herself in front of Emma Kayla let off what sounded like a 'come and get it' growl ending with a distinct snap of her teeth. The mottled gray wolf was pacing back and forth looking for an opening to get past Kayla to Emma. A second wolf, this one a sandy brown joined the gray. Emma doubted Kayla could hold them both off her for long. The back door was only ten feet away from her on the wall she was pressed against. But that ten feet might as well have been ten miles, there was no way she could make it there before they descended on her.

Kayla turned her head and bit down hard on the outside of Emma's wrist. She looked down at her hand, a thick river of blood running down her fingers onto the porch. It didn't even hurt yet. Why was Kayla biting her? They were friends. Then

Kayla gave a little yip, and Emma knew. She wasn't trying to hurt Emma, Kayla was trying to turn her so she had a shot at making it out of this alive. Hoping this was finally her moment, tears slipped unchecked down her cheeks. That's when she felt it. Acid boiling in her blood, coursing through her body. Every nerve was screaming, every single cell sizzling. She didn't feel a wolf inside like she should though. Her body felt full of fire. Knowing it wasn't working she crumpled to her knees. Kian was going to lose her. He couldn't keep fighting if she died. He wouldn't make it. That was not acceptable, damn it! Getting really pissed off at fate, Emma dragged enough air past the burning lava inside to scream as she died.

Her scream ended abruptly with a howl as a russet colored wolf broke free of Emma's skin. Shocked, Emma shook her new body out. It worked? Hell yeah! It worked. Seeing that Kayla had managed to push the two attacking wolves back off the porch Emma jumped with her new body down next to her and growled. Damn, it felt good to be making that noise. These assholes had tried to kill her, they needed to be stopped. So she did, ripping the throat of the mottled one, who smelled like Cathy to her newly enhanced senses, before it even knew what to make of her.

Kayla was shaking the limp body of the sandy brown wolf before tossing it aside. With a brush along Kayla's side as a thank you Emma took off for her mate. Kian was in the thick of it battling it out with three big males. A light colored one was biting into Kian's shoulder, and Emma latched her teeth onto his back and yanked her head to the side ripping the enemy off her mate. The wolf leapt up immediately launching himself at her, using its momentum she knocked it up and over her. Not giving it another chance to attack she bit into its soft under belly.

All the snarling and snapping ended abruptly, and Emma looked around. There were only six wolves still standing including her. Kian looked beautiful, golden wolf with silver eyes blazing. Lifting his head he let out a victorious howl. The sound of his howl echoed through the yard and woods, reverberating off the house back to them. It washed over her in comforting waves. The others tipped their heads back and joined in. Helpless to stop herself Emma let the howl ring up through her throat. It felt glorious.

Chapter 18

As the sound of the howling faded off into the trees, Kian looked at Emma, really looked at her for the first time since the fighting began. He knew she had been turned, had felt the fire through their bond. Her fur a rich russet color, face lightening to a golden cream color. Like the rest of them her eyes were glowing silver. And she had blood on her muzzle. Such a fierce mate. Newly turned and she had fought with more experienced wolves, and won. Kian knew that he was a lucky man, to have the love and loyalty of a woman such as Emma.

This was the pack now gathered around him. Not many were left. The Decker siblings, Lex, Emma and Kian's crew member Jase. Nobody else had stood for him. Kian knew that was thanks to the poison his uncle had spewed for years. His pack may be small, but it was full of wolves that fought and bled beside him. That didn't mean Kian wasn't feeling the loss of so many. Shifters were a rarity, having to hide themselves from the world, and the inherent violence of their lives kept their numbers slim. He wished today had gone differently, he was hopeful it wouldn't have to end this way. These lives were more tragedies on his uncle's list. Shifting back Kian ran his hands through his hair. The fight ended, but there was still much to do today.

When everyone but Emma was standing on two legs again Kian walked over to her. She was sitting there staring at her paws. Remembering how hard it was to find your way back from being a wolf at first Kian knelt down in front of her. "Imagine your wolf tucking back into you. Fingernails instead of claws, the shape of your body, face instead of muzzle." When Emma whined softly at him, he shook his head, understanding. "It won't hurt as much as turning did, I promise. Nothing will ever hurt as much as that." Kian waited patiently until the russet wolf was his woman once again before standing up.

"Who turned you Emma?" he asked. When she shook her head instead of answering him he turned to the others. "Who bit my mate?" This time pushing power into the question.

Kayla angled her head down exposing her neck in a sign of submission. "I did Alpha."

Taking the few steps over to his sister he said "Explain."

"I didn't see another option," Kayla answered eyes still downcast.

"There was a wolf trying to get to me Kian. While Kayla was fighting her a second one came up cornering me. I couldn't get inside to safety," Emma said rushing over to Kayla's side, gripping her hand.

"I knew I couldn't hold them off her forever. They weren't just going to bite her Kian, they wanted to end her. Her chances were better as a wolf, so I bit her."

"And if that killed her instantly?" he asked.

"Then it was better than what they were

171

going to do to her. She means everything to you, but I care about her too, and I couldn't let them do that to her." Finally looking up at her brother Kayla's steel eyes fierce, she finished with, "I am not sorry."

Kian wrapped his little sister in a crushing hug saying, "Thank you for being brave enough to save her."

Kole huffed a small laugh then, "Now you have your wolf Emma, and damn girl, she is a badass."

"At least now I won't be a weak spot for the pack. I can defend myself when I need to," Emma replied.

"Speaking of the pack, I pledge my fealty to you, by tooth and by claw, you are the Alpha. If you will have me," Jase said kneeling down binding himself to Kian like the others all had.

"You fought for me, Jase. You were the only one of the pack other than my family who believed us. You are most welcome in my pack," Kian acknowledged with eyes blazing. "Now, we have to figure all this out," looking at Lex, "any ideas?"

Lex had a plan alright. After everyone grabbed some clothes they brought all of the bodies to Gerald and Cathy's house. It took a few hours to set everything up, thankfully though the pack lived close together, and way outside of town. Setting them in various places in the kitchen and living room. Turned the tv on to the sports channel, and the radio in the kitchen on low. Emma grabbed a frozen pie from the freezer, putting it into the oven to bake. Kole hauled up the old space heater the Wyle's had in their basement, turning it on in the living room. Lex copied everything from Cathy's computer onto the thumb drive he had just to be on the safe side. Kian and Jase wiggled the dryer a bit to loosen the connection on the gas line. By nightfall it would fill the house with enough gas that there would be an explosion big enough that any evidence of the pack's fight would be incinerated. Everyone around town thought that the pack were all a close-knit group of friends, and knew they got together to hang out often. It being

January, in Michigan, most people had space heaters going in their homes, it shouldn't cause any suspicion.

Big fat snowflakes were falling when they got back to Kian's house. Blanketing the yard and further hiding the battle that raged there earlier. While everyone else was heading into the living room, aiming for the dark brown couch Kian went to the kitchen. Hoping to take a little of the strain away he started grabbing things out of the refrigerator. Emma walked in while he was arranging the massive mound of sandwiches on a platter, with a smile for him she grabbed drinks, and together they carried it all into the living room. Everyone was weary, deep down in their bones, but needing to refuel they ate.

Nobody jumped when a little while later they heard the boom. They all knew that it could have easily gone the other way, and it would have been their bodies being disposed of instead of the others. Lex stood up to go. Even off duty, with it being close to his house people would expect him to be on hand. A few minutes later everyone left, heading to their own homes. There was nothing more to do tonight.

Chapter 19

Emma always wondered what it would feel like to have a wolf inside, would it be like an internal monologue, or a like talking to someone else entirely. Turns out it was somewhere in between. There were two distinct halves of her now, although they were both completely Emma. Her wolf saw things from an animal's perspective, operating on a deeply ingrained instinct. Both of them knew Kian was everything important in their world. *Our mate was strong today but he needs us to be soft for him right now.* Listening to her wolf Emma scooted over next to where Kian was seated on the couch. Arms out on either side, his head resting against the back. Wrapping his arm around her Kian pressed Emma into his side. He was staring up at the exposed beams on the ceiling.

"Everything is different now." His voice sounding haunted.

"Yeah. You're the Alpha, and I have a wolf. So much has happened since we met." Emma rested her hand on his chest. Feeling his heart beat slow and steady against her palm.

"Do you regret walking into Dusty's Roadhouse that night?"

Emma knew what he was really asking, but couldn't bring himself to say out loud. Did she regret him? Running her hand up his neck to his cheek she directed him towards her. She wanted his eyes on hers. "The destruction today was put into motion years ago by your uncle, and he left you with no other choice. But I know you're going to be a great Alpha to the pack, *our* pack. As for Kayla turning me, you know I have always wanted that. The circumstances weren't what I would have picked, but I am so glad to have my wolf. She is strong, and makes me feel complete inside. Like she was waiting there all along for the right moment to show herself. And listen, this is the most important part, Kian, I have not regretted a single moment spent with you. How could I? You are the other half of my soul, and I will love you with everything I have in me forever."

Looking into Kian's steel blue eyes she watched him absorb what she said. He was going to give this new pack his all. He was that kind of man, good down to his very marrow. When tears formed in Kian's eyes he closed them and pulled her onto his lap holding on to her tightly, she rested her forehead down on his. Much like he always did, needing to just feel this moment. Through their bond she knew he was struggling to find words to describe how much she meant to him. Shaking her head that he didn't need words, she already knew. The depth of love Kian had inside of him for her was staggering. It was woven into every fiber of his being until Emma was the very air he breathed.

"My beautiful Emma, how did I ever get so lucky? You are the best parts of me. I know I can be a good Alpha because you will be here every step of the way. Everything I am is you, and everything I have is yours. I am honored that you have my back Em, moments after your first turn and you were ripping enemies off me. You are fucking amazing, and I will spend every single day for as long as I am alive being in awe that you're mine."

Tears streaming down her face Emma kissed him. Pressing her lips against his ever so softly. Kian pushed his hands into her heavy waves, cupping the back of her neck. Brushing his tongue across the seam of her lips lightly Emma opened for him. Kian took his time, gliding his tongue over hers, savoring her taste. Needing more, Emma turned her head giving Kian her neck to kiss, and suckle on. "I need, I mean, we need—"

"Me to claim you, I know. My wolf is screaming it at me right now too," he said, interrupting her. His mouth never leaving her neck.

"This is big, if you're not ready we can wait, Kian," Emma moaned.

His hands gliding under the fabric of her shirt pushing it up and over her head, with an arched eyebrow he tossed it away. With one hand he reached behind his head to grab his own shirt yanking it off, while the other was unsnapping her bra. Both items of clothing went the way of her shirt, flying across the room. Kian's lips found her nipple and Emma rocked her hips against him and moaned. His hands busily working on the button and zipper of her jeans. Losing all patience now Emma jumped off him dragging her pants down and kicking out of them. Kian wasted no time in pushing his own jeans down around his ankles.

Dripping wet and past the point of foreplay Emma climbed onto his lap. Taking his dick in her hand she guided it to her entrance. Her eyes locked on his she lowered down onto the length of him. Even after being with him so many times he still stretched her body, he was so big she knew he always would. The blue was gone from his eyes now, leaving them a shining silver, in them she could see her own blazing silver eyes reflecting back at her. Focusing on the bond she started moving slowly up and down on him. Their bodies making a slick sound as he slid in and out of her.

Kian's hands were on her hips, his fingers gripping tight. Like he needed to anchor himself so he wouldn't fly away. She felt his wolf stirring inside and it brought a growl bubbling up her own throat. *Mate, mate, mate*, her wolf was chanting now. Feeling the momentum build Emma sped up rocking her hips against his on each downward stroke. Kian was grunting with each intake of breath. Running her hands into his hair Emma leaned down and pressing her lips against his shoulder said, "Oh, god Kian I'm almost there."

She felt his hands glide up her back to her shoulders as Kian leaned his head down. The scrape of his teeth on her skin left Emma whimpering for more. Knowing what was coming had her body seizing up, clenching his dick. At the first pulse of her orgasm his teeth sank into her chest just below her collar bone. Crying out Emma bit down hard onto his shoulder. Feeling his own orgasm shooting warmth into her she bucked erratically on him.

Kian licked her wound gently. "I claim you as my mate Emma."

Looking down into the eyes of the only man

she would ever love, her body still tingling, she repeated his words. "I claim you as my mate. Nobody but you, Kian. Nobody but you."

Thank you for reading Kian and Emma's story, I hope you love them as much as I do.

~Cara

About the Author

Hi, thanks for reading my book!

Hi, I'm Cara, which is my pen name, but I think of Cara as the most intimate and genuine part of who I am. I live in Michigan with my family, and our fabulously sassy dog. I drink far too much coffee, read all the books I can, hoard makeup, swear more than my mother would like, and dance around my kitchen -poorly- while I cook.

Find me on social media @CaraRomanAuthor! I have zero chill, and LOVE to connect with my readers. It's kind of the best thing ever.

Other Books By Cara Roman

Running From The Wolf (Big Woods Pack Book Two)

The second book in the Big Woods Pack series, Kayla Decker spent years being mad at Lex Kolter. Using her anger as a shield to keep Lex at bay isn't working so well since the shake ups in the pack. Just when they stop fighting each other new information comes to light threatening the pack once again.

Still Yours

High school sweethearts, Ridge left Leigha shortly after graduation to follow his dreams of a career in the music business. Finding his success, but missing home, he is back twelve years later trying to earn a second chance with Leigha. Ridge isn't some eighteen-year-old teenager anymore, a lot has changed. Can Leigha open up and trust her heart to the man who broke it all those years ago?

Definitely Memorable

Caitlyn has always dreamed of vacationing in Ireland. After a disappointing divorce she decides it's time she does something for herself. What she didn't count on was meeting a charming and devastatingly handsome Irishman, Nolan in a pub. Unable, or unwilling, to deny the chemistry between them she throws caution to the wind embarking on a whirlwind romance. Love is never as simple as it seems though, and hers takes a course she never could have predicted.

Other Books From Baying Hound Media

Tell-Tale Hearts
by H.A. Blackwood

Darcy Ford is coming off an ill-advised relationship that ended in disaster. When she's at her lowest point, she meets a woman who takes her back ten years to a night of wild passion. A night when she met-and lost-someone who opened new worlds to her. A night where her heart was stolen. A night which was the beginning of this most recent disastrous affair. Only by re-telling these tales can she find her way back to her lost love and the return of her heart.

Candid Camera
by H.A. Blackwood

A new relationship. A secret from the past. Will their love survive?
Darcy Ford and Gemma Amante are contemplating the next big move in their relationship when Ashleigh, a lover from Gemma's past, shows up unexpectedly. She brings news that has Darcy and Gemma on a trip to Los Angeles.

Gemma's friends from her old life as a sex worker are in trouble and need help. Going undercover as sex cam workers in the city of sin may seem like a literal pleasure trip, but when they go up against a new type of criminal, they're going to need all of their sexy savvy. Between steamy escapades, clues begin to emerge. If they're going to solve this mystery, they'll have to risk their way of life, their relationship, and their very lives.

Adored: A Collection Of Poetry
Volume One
by H.A. Blackwood

Whimsical. Fantastical. Celestial.

The poems in this book reflect a lot of different things, but they all have one thing in common: you'll wish they were written about you. You'll wish this was a permanent tribute to you, the reader, on display for the world to see.

Such is the magic of the written word. It can bring out many emotions, but the one you'll be left with after reading this book is simply this: adored.